W9-BSO-534

Kiss Me, Janie Tannenbaum

Books by Elizabeth-Ann Sachs:

Just Like Always
I Love You, Janie Tannenbaum
A Special Kind of Friend
Kiss Me, Janie Tannenbaum

Kiss Me, Janie Tannenbaum

Elizabeth-Ann Sachs

A JEAN KARL BOOK

Atheneum   1992   New York

Maxwell Macmillan Canada
Toronto

Maxwell Macmillan International
New York   Oxford   Singapore   Sydney

Atheneum
Macmillan Publishing Company
866 Third Avenue
New York, NY 10022

Maxwell Macmillan Canada, Inc.
1200 Eglinton Avenue East
Suite 200
Don Mills, Ontario M3C 3N1

Macmillan Publishing Company is part of the Maxwell Communication
Group of Companies.

First edition
Printed in the United States of America
10 9 8 7 6 5 4 3 2 1
The text of this book is set in 12 point Caledonia.
Book design by Tania Garcia

Library of Congress Cataloging-in-Publication Data

Sachs, Elizabeth-Ann.
Kiss me, Janie Tannenbaum/Elizabeth-Ann Sachs.—1st ed.
p.   cm.
"A Jean Karl book."
Summary: Janie gains a new perspective on boys when she and her
boy-crazy best friend go on a whale-watching expedition.
ISBN 0-689-31664-X
[1. Whale watching—Fiction.   2. Whales—Fiction.   3. Friendship —
Fiction.]   I. Title.
PZ7.S1186Ki   1992
[Fic]—dc20   91-28465

To my father,
who taught me to love and respect
not only the sea
but all of the natural world

CHAPTER 1

"ARE you ready?" said Harold Wazby.

Janie Tannenbaum crouched forward on the three-legged stool. She leaned against the cow's massive side, which rose and fell with the animal's breathing. Fern smelled of sweet hay and sour milk. "Okay, Harold, now I'm set."

Fern stamped the old barn floor. Puffs of dust rose up.

"Easy, girl," Janie said rubbing her fingers to warm them. "Easy, girl. Let's hope Fern is ready too."

Harold leaned on the stall gate and began reading: " 'It was the best of times, it was the worst of times, it was the age of wisdom, it was the age of foolishness . . .' " He paused.

"Go on," Janie said. "She likes it."

" '. . . it was the season of Light, it was the season of Darkness . . .' "

Janie's hands worked the cow's soft teats with a steady tugging motion. Jets of warm milk shot out in rhythmic blasts and drummed inside the pail.

Fern shifted her hindquarters. One hoof stamped dangerously close to the milk pail. "Easy, girl. Ea-sy."

"Should I keep going?"

"Yes!"

" '. . . we had everything before us, we had nothing before us . . .' "

Janie began milking her neighbor Mr. Ransom's cows the summer she saw a calf born. As part of the milking, Mr. Ransom said the cows liked being read to. He left *A Tale of Two Cities* and other books on a shelf in a corner of the barn. At first Janie didn't believe it would make a difference, but whenever Harold read, Fern and Zelda stopped behaving like bucking broncos.

Janie sat up straight. "Okay, I'm just about done."

Harold pushed his glasses up on his nose. He scratched between Fern's small horns. "Wonder how it could have been the best and worst time at the same time?"

"Who knows, but it kept her quiet."

"How'd she do?"

"Good! She gave plenty of milk."

On their way out, Janie left milk for the barn cats, then closed the heavy wooden doors and waited while Harold placed the pails in a special shed near the Ransoms' house. She was going to miss these evening milkings.

They crossed the dirt road, climbed over a crumbling stone wall, then cut through a rocky Connecticut pasture. A winding trail led down to the pine woods that surrounded the lake.

Their favorite spot was a narrow flat rock jutting into the water, perfect for fishing and skipping stones. Harold had dubbed it "Hippo's Back" long ago. The best time of day was sunset, when the water turned golden.

"So," said Harold, "when are you leaving?"

Janie moved out to the sunny end of the rock. "For vacation or school?"

"Both."

"Sunday night we'll be hoisting the mains'il, clapping on the ratlines . . ."

"Could you run that by me in English?"

Janie laughed. Ever since her parents had decided to take her whale watching, she'd been boning up on

3

her seafaring words. "Sunday, we'll be setting sail from Cape Cod."

"Are you coming back afterward?"

"For a few days. Then I leave for Courtney's and my parents take off." Janie didn't like thinking about her mother and father being gone for almost a year. She raised her arms and bellowed, "Oh, the briny deep!"

The lake was smooth as a marble cut in half. Nothing rustled in the underbrush. No birds called out. It was too early for the gnats to start biting or for the bullfrogs' serenade.

In the middle of the lake, a small sunfish jumped out of the water. "Thar she blows," cried Janie.

"I should've brought my fishing rod," Harold said.

"I wish you'd brought your flute. Why bother with the fish? Most of them are too little."

"You don't have to keep them, Janie."

It *was* neat, Janie thought, the way Harold always threw fish back. Even the big ones. He'd ease the hook out of the fish's mouth so it wouldn't rip open the lip, and he did it all underwater so the fish could breath.

Harold sat down. Janie crouched next to him and peered into the still, clear shallows. Her freckled face and curly red hair floated next to his on the surface of the water. She never thought of Harold as handsome, but with his summer tan and curly dark hair, he looked great.

Beneath the water, one fat bluegill nosed its way through the reeds. Janie tapped Harold's shoulder and pointed. He studied the shallows then looked at her. "See if you can do it," she said.

Very, very slowly Harold eased his hand into the lake. Without making a ripple, his fingers slid around the reeds where the bluegill was feeding.

Harold's long slender thumb reached out. The fish shot away into deeper water.

"Oh, too bad!" said Janie.

"I almost touched him."

"I wonder if anyone ever caught fish that way, Harold?"

"My lore book says the Indians lulled fish by stroking their bellies."

Harold stretched out on his back. He put his hands behind his head and crossed his legs at the ankles.

"Before you leave for vacation, we should do something."

"Sure. What do you want to do?"

"Something special."

"Harold, remember what we did before I went into the hospital?"

Sunlight sparkled on Harold's glasses. Janie couldn't see his eyes. A smile crept across his face. "You still got the scar we made, Harold?"

He held up his left index finger. The scar was small and pale but still there.

Janie rubbed the scar on her finger. "Do you still have that scout knife we used? Not one of the books said anything about blood-brother pacts hurting."

"There was blood all over the snow." He laughed. "It looked like someone died out here. But I don't want to do that again."

"Yeah, it's not a good idea to be mixing blood these days."

"That's not what I was thinking of anyway, Janie."

"So what do you want to do, then?"

"Go to the movies."

"Sure. Last Saturday was super."

"No, just you and me. Not a whole gang."

Janie frowned. "What'd you mean? Like going out?"

Harold sat up. "No, but I thought we could go Saturday night."

"We're not allowed to bike into town after dark."

"Oh, right."

"Harold, the county fair! I heard they've got a three-hundred-pound chicken this year."

"Get out!"

"Okay, mabe it's only two hundred pounds."

"Let's do that."

Harold wrapped his arms around his legs and stared at the lake. "I can't believe you're going into seventh at Courtney's school, Janie."

"I'm not ready to start thinking about school. Come on, I'll race you home."

After dinner Mrs. Tannenbaum said, "Listen, troops, we've got to start packing up this house."

"Awh, Mom, let's do it when we come back from vacation."

Janic's father nodded. "We'll have a week to get Janie ready for Courtney's and close up the house. That should be enough time."

"Well," said Mrs. Tannenbaum. "I guess we can manage, if we all work on it."

"Tell you what," Janie's father said. "Let's make lists. If we're organized, it won't seem so awful." He reached for a pad of paper and a pen on the sideboard.

Janie shot cookie crumbs across the table while her parents discussed camera equipment. For the next ten months, they would be traveling all over the world, filming a TV documentary on endangered animals in the wild.

Mr. Tannenbaum said, "There's probably lots of gear we don't need to take."

"Right," said Janie's mother.

"I still wish I could go with you guys instead of living at Courtney's. I mean, it'll be fun and all, but . . . I want to be with you."

"I know." Mrs. Tannenbaum nodded. "The director did say he'll try to squeeze you in over the winter holidays."

"But suppose he can't?"

Janie's father said, "We'll get you there, wherever we are. I promise."

"Okay," she sighed.

Janie's little brown poodle whined at her feet. He sat on his hind legs, begging.

"What is it, Fang?" His tail wagged. Janie slipped him a cookie.

The phone rang. "I'll get it." Janie ran down the hall. Fang charged after her.

"Ahh-oy, sailor!" Janie said as she heard laughter at the other end of the line. "Courtney! I was just talking about you."

"Oh, Janie, I'm so excited. I can't believe I'm really going out on the ocean for four days."

Janie had been surprised when Courtney actually accepted the invitation to go whale watching. Usually,

Courtney's idea of roughing it was riding a crowded bus across New York City. She considered a picnic in Central Park an outdoor adventure. It was amazing how they liked one another though. Ever since they shared a hospital room and surgery for scoliosis three years ago, they'd been best friends.

"Janie, are you there?"

"Yeah."

"Do you think they'll have plenty of life preservers on board. I was watching this old movie where a boat didn't have enough and the people—"

"Courtney, are you sure you want to come?"

"Oh, Janie, yes. It'll be good for me."

"What do you mean?"

"I was reading how important it is to be in tune with nature . . ."

Janie slid down the wall until she hit the floor. She stretched out her legs, getting comfortable. Fang curled up at her feet.

". . . I mean, I want to commune with the natural world like you do."

"What?"

"Oh, you know. Being in the woods every day, milking cows. It's so wonderfully rugged and outdoorsy."

"Well, okay."

"So, should I bring an extra life preserver?"

"Just warm clothing, it gets cold."

"Nothing dressy?"

"Nope."

"Oh—Janie, guess what happened!"

"What's that?"

"I got it."

"It?" said Janie.

"You know! *It!*"

"Oh, *that* it! Was it gross?"

"No. All that stuff about cramps and feeling sick. It's not true. I feel like—I don't know—wonderful."

"I can wait."

"And Janie, there's more."

"Yeah?"

"Remember that boy, Mark, who goes to my school? He really likes me."

"How do you know?"

"I sort of went out with him yesterday."

"What'd you do?"

"Met him at the movies."

"What'd you see?"

"Janie! He kissed me!"

"Jeez, why'd he do that?"

"He really likes me."

"I wouldn't be caught dead kissing a boy, except

Fang. I kiss him on the lips all the time." Janie petted the dog's head.

Courtney laughed. "That's disgusting, Janie Tannenbaum, but maybe you'll change your mind when you come here. There're lots of cute boys in my school."

"I don't think so. It wouldn't feel like me if I did."

CHAPTER 2

SATURDAY afternoon, Janie and Harold took the bus into town. It let them off across the street from the entrance to the county fair. As they waited for the lights to change, the smells of horses and straw and cotton candy drifted toward them.

"Harold, we have to do the roller coaster. Oh, and the Whirlwind. We never got to it last year."

"The one everyone says makes you throw up?"

"That's it, Harold."

"I don't believe it's that bad."

"Bet we could do it ten times and we wouldn't get sick."

Harold grinned. "Hey! You want to?"

"Sure! What you think?"

Inside the grounds, they wandered through different tents, looking at prize bulls, plow horses, and giant pumpkins. Mrs. Ransom had won a blue ribbon for her apple pie.

Near the track, a tall man in a mustard-colored suit shouted, "This way to the dog races. Get your tickets here. Next race, fifteen minutes."

Somewhere in the distance a band played old-fashioned waltzing music. Friends called out to one another.

Harold pointed to a man packing waffle cones with ice cream. "Want one, Janie?"

"Yeah." She licked her lips. "All these smells are making me hungry."

"What flavor?"

"Coffee. Here's some money."

"My treat." Harold walked away before Janie could pull a dollar out of her pocket.

"Okay," she called after him, "but I buy next time."

They ate their ice cream standing in front of the pigpen. A fat momma pig and her youngsters snuffled for handouts at the fence.

"Hi, guys." Janie bent down. She scratched the black-and-white pig's bristly snout.

Harold crouched beside her. "Know what I read, Janie? Dogs were the first animals domesticated by humans. And pigs were next."

"Gee, I would have thought cows came before pigs."

"That's what this book at school said."

"Hey, you got chocolate on you."

"Where?" Harold rubbed his cheek.

"Down here." Janie licked her bottom lip.

Harold licked his lower lip. "Did I get it all? I don't want to look like a nerd."

Janie rubbed off the last bit with her thumb. "Oh!" she said. Harold's lip was warm like the cow's teats.

"What?"

"Nothing. Let's hit the rides."

First they took the ghost train through the haunted castle, where they banged into skeletons and were charged by headless knights. Near the end, giant spiders tried to trample them.

"That was so fake," Janie said as they came through the exit. "You could see the motors inside those spiders."

"I saw you covering your face, Janie. You were scared."

"No way, Harold! What's next?"

"The Tunnel of Love."

"Now, that's scary."

"You big baby!"

"How about the Whirlwind?"

"Okay, and then after that the Tunnel of Love."

"Get out, Harold."

They strolled along the midway until they saw the Whirlwind in the distance. It was a simple-looking roller coaster, just one circle about five stories high. It didn't have any dangerous curves or sharp plunges. However, the train you rode was on the inside of the circle, so that the riders, when they reached the top, were hanging upside down in the open cars.

"How come they don't fall out?" Janie shouted. The ride slowed near the top. People screamed.

"Centrifugal force or something. You ready? I'll get the tickets."

"Let me, Harold. It's my turn."

"All right, all right."

"We want to ride it ten times," Janie said to the man inside the booth.

"What are you—nuts?" he shouted through the little window. "You wanna die?"

"We can do it."

"Well, then you got forty bucks, kid?"

Janie looked at Harold. "We don't have enough money. Want to try it twice and see if we can get sick on that?"

"Sure." He laughed.

They were the first ones on the Whirlwind. Janie gripped the bar and braced herself against the seat.

Harold did the same. The guard made sure the safety catch was locked.

Janie refused to close her eyes as the Whirlwind began to move. The train roared to the top. Centrifugal force, centrifugal force, Janie kept thinking as her stomach lurched and quivered. She gritted her teeth and tried not to think about falling.

The Whirlwind plunged. The lights of the fairground swirled into lines of red and blue. The wind whistled in her eyes.

It went around again and then again. The world rolled by in waves. Harold's eyes were closed.

They jerked to a halt. "I feel seasick," Janie said.

With one hand clinging to the seat, Harold fumbled putting on his glasses. "I do too, a little. If you want to pass on the second ride, that's okay."

Harold looked gray to Janie. "Yeah, my stomach could use a rest."

Janie and Harold found the quiet end of the fairground where small children rode the carousel and the Ferris wheel. They sat on a bench and listened to the music.

"We're going to have to go soon, Harold."

"I'm pretty sure we can use those two leftover tickets for another ride."

"Do you want to?"

"Yup."

16

"You pick then."

Harold grinned. "Tunnel of Love!"

"Harold!"

"Okay. Okay. The Ferris wheel."

They climbed into the metal bucket seat. An attendant lowered the bar across their laps to block them from standing. "Now, don't fool around, kids."

Harold patted Janie on the head. "I'll make sure my little sister stays put."

Janie elbowed him in the ribs. "We won't."

The Ferris wheel began to move. It rotated slowly. Harold clamped both hands on the guardrail and pushed his weight against it. The bucket seat rocked back and forth. He did it again.

"Hey, neat." Janie pressed against the railing too. "Do it with me, Harold."

They pushed together and the seat swung way out and back. "It's like being in a baby cradle." Janie laughed.

The Ferris wheel halted. They were at the highest point. Harold put his arm across the top of the seat. Janie leaned back. The warmth of his arm against her shoulders felt good.

Pink and orange stripes lined the sky. The clouds were purple splotches. Janie looked off in the direction of Ransoms' farm. It was too far away to see.

Harold tugged on one of her curls and let it go.

He did it again. "Is your hair always going to be curly like this?"

Janie shrugged. "I don't know."

He coiled a strand around his finger. Then he leaned over toward her. "Janie."

"What?" Harold's face looked odd. He tilted his head in close to hers.

Oh, no! He was going to kiss her. "Hey, look at that!" She pointed.

Startled, he turned away. "What?"

"That sky. I mean, isn't it great?"

"Yeah, nice sunset." He turned back. "Janie."

This time she could feel his breath on her forehead. He smelled of ice cream and sweat and laundry soap. It was a funny combination.

He moved even closer.

"Harold! Quit it."

"Why?"

"Because!"

"Because why, Janie?"

"Because, because, I don't know."

Harold pulled his arm away. He stared off at the sky.

Boy, thought Janie. Why'd he have to go and do that? He was spoiling everything.

The Ferris wheel began to move down slowly. A

chilly breeze took the warmth from Janie's shoulder where Harold's arm had been. She shivered.

"Listen," she said. "Could we talk about Fang?"

Harold said nothing.

"Is it okay if I bring him over real early tomorrow before we leave?"

Harold folded his arms across his chest. "Yeah, sure," he said. "No problem."

CHAPTER 3

A DRY hot wind blew up Courtney's block, dusting the cars parked bumper to bumper along the curb. In a couple of weeks, Janie thought, she'd be living here without any cows or woods around her. At least there was the Hudson River glittering with sunlight just down the street.

Janie opened the back door of the station wagon. "I'll get Courtney."

"The doorman'll let the Schaeffers know we're here," said Janie's mother. "We're not going upstairs. There's no place to park."

"Aww, really." Janie loved the view of the river from Courtney's living room windows.

"Hi, Janie."

"Hey!"

Courtney's long blond hair fell around her shoulders. Little pink, white, and gold star earrings dangled at her neck. She was dressed in a pink shirt, baggy white shorts, and white sandals. Janie was sure Courtney could be a teen model.

Courtney hugged her. She kept her arm around Janie's waist. "I can't believe I'm really doing this." Janie laughed. "Last chance to back out."

"No way," said Courtney.

The doorman piled Courtney's luggage in the back of the car. Janie said, "I think you have as much for the four days as I will for the entire school year."

"You know me. I couldn't make up my mind what to wear, so I brought everything. Even my sketchbook and pastels in case the whales don't show."

"Oh, man," said Janie, "they better."

Courtney's mother came through the revolving door wearing a shiny green dress and high heels. She was the only person Janie knew who always dressed as if she were on her way to a party. "Hi, Mrs. Schaeffer."

"How are you, dear?"

"Good," Janie said.

"I want the two of you to be careful on board that boat. Don't get too close to the edge."

"We will," said Janie. "I mean, we won't."

"Courtney, did you pack your seasickness medication?"

"Yes."

"All aboard, that's going aboard," said Janie's father.

"Bye." Courtney kissed her mother. She climbed in the backseat next to Janie. "I'm so glad to be getting away from here. I spent the whole night crying. Do I look really terrible?"

"No, why? What happened?"

Janie's mother opened the front door. "We'll see you Thursday night."

"I'll tell you later," Courtney whispered.

"Take care." Mrs. Schaeffer waved.

Janie rolled down the window. "We'll bring back a whale for you."

They traveled all day. Janie and Courtney were never alone in the car or during the picnic lunch. Even when Janie's father stopped for gas, Janie's mother went to the rest room with them.

Finally, late in the afternoon, Mr. Tannenbaum parked in a boat marina near Gloucester, Massachusetts. Janie and Courtney piled out.

"Look." Courtney pointed.

A large gray seagull coasted across the sky. His shrill cries pierced the early evening quiet.

"Let's go down to the dock," Janie said.

"Don't be long!" said Mrs. Tannenbaum. "We have to unload."

"We'll be right back. Come on, Courtney." Janie led the way in between the cars, across a sandy parking lot, and down the gangway to the pier. Yachts and schooners and tugs were tied up all along the dock. On a houseboat, an old man threw hunks of bread into the water. The seagulls fought each other for it.

"Nice manners," Courtney said.

"Hey—why were you upset before?"

"Oh, I'd almost forgotten." Courtney looked at her hands. "Remember I told you about Mark?"

"Yeah?"

"My friend Margeurite saw him kissing some girl at the movies."

"Boy—does that stink!"

"I thought he really liked me, Janie. That's why I let him kiss me. I don't know how he could do that."

Janie watched a gull diving out of the sky. "Yeah, everything's getting so weird. Harold wanted to kiss me yesterday, but I wouldn't do it."

"Janie! Why not? He likes you so much!"

"I don't know."

"Do you think he'll start hanging around with some other girl?"

Janie laughed. "No way."

"Oh, you're so lucky."

Janie looked at Courtney. "I mean, I don't think he would."

Courtney tossed her hair off her shoulder. "Well, I can tell you one thing for sure. I don't care if Mark begs me, I'd never go out with him now."

"I don't blame you."

"Getting your 'sea legs,' ladies?" Mr. Tannenbaum stepped carefully as he came down the gangway.

"Right," said Janie.

"We better get our things down here. It looks like people are starting to gather."

The Tannenbaums and Courtney made two trips each and piled all their gear on the dock. By the time they finished, a crowd of thirty was milling around. As Janie and Courtney slipped up to the front, they heard a family speaking in Japanese and two people speaking in French.

"Attention, everyone!" A deeply tanned heavyset man faced the crowd. He held a clipboard under his arm. "May I have everyone's attention, please! I'm Captain Bob Rafford, and we'll be going aboard the *Yankee* in a few minutes. I'd like to welcome you all and introduce a few people. Ted, here on my right, is first mate. You won't see much of him after we shove off. He'll be up in the wheelhouse navigating."

Ted, a small bald man, nodded. "Evening folks."

Captain Bob looked around. "Where's Pete?"

"I'm over here." Pete waved. He was tall like the captain but had a reddish beard.

"Pete's one of the naturalist guides for the trip. You'll meet Vicky, the other guide, on board. They'll be telling you more about whales than you ever wanted to know."

Everyone laughed. Someone whistled.

The captain looked around. "Steve?"

"Here!" A stocky boy with sun bleached hair stood at the edge of the crowd. His faded blue T-shirt had two whales on it.

Courtney smiled at Janie. "Oh, my."

"Great shirt," said Janie.

"Steve is studying to be a naturalist guide. But since he's also my son, he's taking additional training in the kitchen."

The people around Janie laughed. She liked the way Steve nodded and pretended to push a broom.

"Ralph and Monica?" The captain called out.

"We're here," said a man with skin so pale he looked as if he'd never been in the sun. He stood beside a girl with big brown eyes and straight dark hair. She had on a T-shirt just like the captain's son.

"Ralph and Monica," the captain said, "are your galley crew. They'll be responsible for meals and will be serving a light supper once we're under way."

The captain looked at his clipboard. "I have a few announcements before we shove off. On board you will find ladders on the port and starboard sides of the dining room leading below to cabins. Single women are bunking in Cabin Four. It sleeps eight, so it's a bit tight. Single men are in Cabin Seven—same idea. Couples and families check with Steve. Crew gets the floor in the dining area."

Janie heard a few laughs around her.

The captain looked up and nodded. "As you're already guessing, this is not a luxury liner. Cramped quarters at best, but most of your time will be spent on deck. There are two showers, near the galley, for everyone, so be considerate. And be sure to conserve water."

Courtney whispered, "How old do you think Steve is?"

Janie shrugged.

"Also," the captain continued. "Please make sure you wear tie-shoes with rubber soles on board. No loose fitting sandals. It can get pretty rough out there, and we don't want anyone slipping."

"This is like going to sea for real," Janie said.

Courtney clutched her shoulder bag. "I'm getting that feeling."

"Welcome aboard, then," said Captain Bob. "We hope you enjoy your trip."

When Janie and Courtney reached the gangway, Steve was standing there. "Hi. Need a hand?"

"No, thanks," Janie said, but she fumbled and dropped her whale book.

"Hey—" Steve handed it back. "I have this. It's the best."

"My parents gave it to me. They're doing a documentary on endangered animals."

"Pete and Vicky'll want to meet them. Well . . ." Steve paused as if he didn't know what else to say.

Courtney tossed her hair off her shoulder. "Hi, I'm Courtney Schaeffer and this is Janie Tannenbaum. I'd love some help with my suitcases." She handed over two and let Steve lead the way up on deck. Over her shoulder, she winked at Janie.

Janie hoisted up her duffel bag and followed. Sometimes Courtney acted really goofy.

CHAPTER 4

THE ladder ran straight up the wall. Janie stood at the bottom of it looking up at Courtney. "You have to come down facing the wall. Be careful, the rungs are narrow."

"What about my luggage?"

"Throw it down first."

Janie stepped aside as three soft suitcases came flying toward her. Then Courtney teetered unsteadily from one rung to another.

Below, there was only a small passageway with four curtained doors. At one end was a sink the size of a large cooking pot.

"Here we are, Cabin Two." Janie pulled open the curtain.

"Janie, it's so tiny! I thought it would be like those cruise ships you see on TV."

Janie said, "I was hoping to sleep in a hammock like they did in old sailor movies."

Before them was a space less than six feet long and four feet wide. Two bunks hung one over the other with barely enough room between them and the wall to turn around.

Courtney followed Janie inside. "What'll we do with our stuff?"

"Beats me. Unless we throw it overboard." Janie tossed her backpack and books on the upper bunk.

"Janie! Where's our bathroom?"

Janie shrugged. "I guess we don't have one."

"You mean we have to share with other people?" Courtney looked around. "There's not even a mirror!"

Janie hoisted herself onto the top cot. Her legs hung over the edge. "You don't need a mirror now that you're becoming a sailor. The whales won't care if you don't wear makeup. They'll fall in love with you anyway."

Courtney dropped her suitcases on the floor. "I wish someone would."

"Hey, forget Mark! You're going to have a terrific time."

Courtney nodded. "You're right! It's like we're back sharing a hospital room, only better, there's no hospital."

Janie smiled remembering the pranks she and Courtney had pulled. Their best had been trying to fix up a doctor and a nurse. "Remember the mysterious pigeon lady and how we fed the pigeons that gross food?"

"I can't believe we really threw food out our windows. No wonder Mrs. Bickerstaff was always charging into our room. Janie, do you think we could change to a cabin that has a bathroom?"

"Hey! We don't even have a porthole! Now that's something to complain about."

"Let's ask Steve."

Janie leaned over and pressed her ear against the wall. "Our cabin must be in the middle of the boat. Maybe the next cabin over has a porthole."

"Janie."

"What?"

"Do you think he's cute?"

"Who?"

"Steve!"

"What are you talking about?"

"Steve! Isn't he cute?"

Janie sat up straight. "Well, his hair's the same color as a golden retriever's. That's sort of neat."

"Oh, come on. He's so rugged looking." Courtney placed her shoulder bag on the lower cot and unzipped it.

"If you say so."

Courtney began brushing her hair. "Janie, I'm really glad I decided to do this. We're going on a whole new adventure, setting out into the world. We're like women explorers."

Janie rolled her eyes.

The boat's engine started up with a roar. The entire vessel vibrated with the noise.

Courtney grabbed for the edge of the cot. Janie shouted, "Let's go up on deck."

"I have to put on sneakers first." Holding onto her bunk, Courtney reached for her bag on the floor.

Janie shoved it toward her, thinking that Courtney was going to need extra help getting used to life on the open seas.

Janie and Courtney climbed up the ladder to the main deck. They walked through a long room with windows on both sides. Beneath the windows were booths with built-in tables. A large center aisle ran between the booths.

"Guess this is where we eat," Janie said.

The galley kitchen was at the back of the boat. Almost the same size, Janie thought, as her bedroom closet. Every pot and pan was clamped in place. Probably things crashed and rolled once the boat was under way. Janie didn't point that out to Courtney.

"Look at the sign on this door, Janie. It says Head."

"You found the bathroom!"

"All the way up here! What about in the middle of the night?"

"No problem!" Janie laughed. "All you have to do is roll out of bed, climb up the ladder, walk the length of the boat, try not to fall overboard and be eaten by giant squid, and you're there."

"Swell!" Courtney opened the door. "At least it's got a mirror."

"Hey, check out the sign over the sink. We have to wash in salt water."

"Janie! There's no tub! Not even a shower stall."

Janie spotted a drain in the tile floor and a shower faucet over the toilet. "Up there," she pointed. "Guess you just stand next to the toilet and let it hit you."

"I don't know about this. Just the idea of washing in salt water makes me itchy. Maybe I'll use extra perfume and skip it for a few days."

"Way to go, Courtney!" Janie patted her on the shoulder. "I'll make a slob out of you yet."

"Let's go find your parents."

The sun had set. The smell of gasoline and fish mingled with the salty air. Overhead gulls circled.

Though the boat's engines hummed, the *Yankee* hadn't left the dock.

Moored next to the *Yankee* was a small houseboat. Inside, a woman watched a cowboy movie.

On another, larger vessel, a group of people posed with their fish as they waited for the camera to flash. One man held a cod over his wide-open mouth. It looked as though he were going to swallow it.

Janie's parents stood at the stern, the wide back end of the boat. "All settled?" her father asked.

"We threw everything on the floor. My kind of place, not even any hangers to mess with."

Janie's mother shook her head. "Can this be my child?" She looked at Janie's father, who shrugged.

"Dad, do you guys have a porthole?"

"No, why?"

"We were wondering if we could change cabins to one that does."

"And maybe," Courtney added, "has a cute little bathroom of its own."

"I don't think so." Mrs. Tannenbaum shook her head. "I'm pretty sure we took the last cabins when we signed up."

"And besides"— Janie's father leaned against the railing—"the *Yankee*'s nothing more than an over-grown tugboat. All the cabins are small and on the lower deck. Probably none of them have portholes or bathrooms. But then most of our time will be spent hanging around on this deck or the upper one."

"What's up there?" Janie said.

"The wheelhouse, captain's quarters, and a wide-open area for watching whales."

Courtney shielded her eyes and looked up. "Any bathrooms?"

"Just in the captain's quarters, but that's off limits."

"Look," said Mrs. Tannenbaum. "We're casting off."

A man on the dock unwound a large coil of rope wrapped around a metal cleat. He threw the line onto the deck, moved to the next cleat, and did the same thing. On deck another crew member neatly rewound each line.

From up in the wheelhouse, two blasts signaled departure. The *Yankee* slid away from the pier.

"Woa," said Janie. "We're moving."

Courtney gripped the railing. "I've never been anywhere but on land."

The gap between the dock and the boat widened. Janie said, "It feels like the land is backing away from us."

"It does," said Mrs. Tannenbaum.

The boat eased between tall wooden pilings where

beady-eyed gulls sat watching. Heading out of the harbor, the *Yankee* passed the rows and rows of boats moored in their slips.

Bye, Fang. Bye, Harold, Janie thought.

"Hello there," said a voice. It was Pete, the naturalist guide. Steve was right behind him.

"Hiya, guys," Janie said.

"Hello," Courtney sang. Her star earrings twinkled.

Pete said, "Steve's been telling me about your parents, Janie. Are they around?"

Janie turned. "Mom. Dad."

Pete reached out to shake hands with Mr. and Mrs. Tannenbaum. "News travels fast aboard ship. I hear you're doing a documentary on endangered animals?"

Janie's father said, "We are."

Pete began talking with Janie's parents. Steve stood with his arms crossed, legs apart, listening.

The *Yankee* tooted its horn again as a small tug chugged past, heading toward the pier. Janie waved to the man on deck.

Courtney nudged her. "Do I look all right?" she whispered.

"What?" said Janie.

Courtney leaned closer to Janie. "I wanted to know if—"

"Your attention, please!" The captain's voice came over the loudspeaker. "We'll have our first whale lecture in about an hour in the dining room. Please plan to attend."

Pete said, "We'd better get going, Steve. It was good talking with you folks. I hope there's time to chat once we're under way."

"Yes," Mrs. Tannenbaum said. "We want to learn all we can while we're here."

Pete pointed to the front of the boat. "There's a drawbridge up ahead. If you stand on the bowsprit—the narrow part sticking out of the front—you'll have the best view."

"I want to see that," Janie said.

"Bye, Pete. Bye, Steve," said Courtney. Steve did a mock salute and hurried after Pete.

Courtney watched him move along the deck. "He's even got a sailor's walk, Janie."

"Let's head toward the bow," Mr. Tannenbaum said.

Janie and Courtney followed. Courtney said, "Do you think he noticed me?"

"You should ask him."

"Janie!"

"Okay, I guess you can't."

"Of course not. What do you think?"

"Who knows!"

"Did you see the way he was smiling when he came over? You think that means something?"

"You got me."

"How old do you think he is?"

"Hey, look." Janie pointed. "The bridge is going up."

An hour out of port, the lights of the Boston skyline faded and darkness fell around the *Yankee*. The sea wind whipped against the boat.

"Want to go in?" Courtney said. "I'm cold."

Janie slid open the heavy wooden door that led into the dining area. "Let's grab a booth up front for the talk. We don't want to miss anything."

"Okay." Courtney looked around the room.

Janie sank into the leather seat of the second booth. Her parents were sitting with the Japanese family on the other side of the aisle. Janie waved.

Monica worked her way down the aisle with a tray on her hip. "Meatloaf sandwich?"

"Sure," Janie said. "Two."

Courtney unfolded her paper napkin. "Is there something hot to drink?"

"I'll be bringing chocolate, coffee, and tea around in a little while."

Janie took a bite of her sandwich. "Mmm."

When everyone had settled down, Pete flicked the lights off, then flicked them back on. The talking ceased. Steve crept down the aisle and stood beside Pete.

"First," Pete said, "we'd like to give you an idea of what to expect. Each day'll start when the sun comes up or when the first whale is sighted. If you want to sleep late 'cause you're on vacation—feel free. Of course, you'll miss everything, and we'll make fun of you."

Around the room people laughed. There was low conversation.

"Somehow," Pete continued, "we'll fit in meals, and a slide show or lecture each day, but everything comes to a halt when the whales show up. A lot depends on the weather too. The forecast looks good though, so plan on spending most of your time on deck." Pete stroked his beard.

"Now, then, tonight our boat will be cruising through the Gulf of Maine. Because of the warm and cold currents that mix out there, we'll be running into some turbulent waters."

The audience stirred. A few people whispered. Courtney fidgeted with her napkin.

"Not to worry. We've never had a problem yet,

and those churning waters are what draw up food for the whales from the bottom of the ocean. So by morning, you'll be entering what we think of as a 'truck stop' for whales."

Janie laughed. Steve grinned at her.

Pete continued, "My assistant, Vicky, will tell you a little about how whales feed." He stepped aside.

Janie thought of a bird when the small woman with curly black hair stood up. Even her voice was songlike.

Vicky smiled at the group. "Some scientists believe that more than fifty million years ago the ancestors of whales were also the ancestors of deer and antelope. It's believed these creatures left the land for the ocean because there was so much competition for food. Today whales graze for food in herds, much like deer. It takes a lot to feed a fifty-ton whale—a ton of food a day."

"Wow!" Janie slapped a hand over her mouth.

Vicky laughed. "Wow, is right! Especially when you know that some whales eat krill, very small shrimplike crustaceans. They're eating machines. So they have to migrate to where food is most abundant. That's where we're headed."

Even though Vicky had interesting things to say, Janie's mind began to drift. She imagined herself a naturalist guide, being out on the ocean all-year-round.

Courtney leaned closer. "Janie, do you think Steve has a girlfriend?"

Janie looked around. Maybe it wasn't too late to get another meatloaf sandwich.

CHAPTER 5

JANIE awoke to the sound of sloshing water and the creaking of wooden timbers. Like a giant cradle, she thought, as the boat rocked from side to side.

Although the cabin was dark, Janie guessed that it must be morning. She sat part way up, resting on her elbows.

"Courtney, you awake?"

No answer.

Janie unzipped her sleeping bag and threw it open. Last night she'd decided it was impossible to change into pajamas in such a little space, so she'd slept in her clothes.

Now all she had to do was put on her sneakers. Janie climbed down from her cot, stumbled around Courtney's three suitcases, and crept out. In the hall, she tied up her laces.

As she came up on deck, harsh clear sunlight stung her eyes. Janie took deep breaths of cold salty air.

As far as her eyes could see, whichever way she looked, only water was visible. Dark sparkling water rolled on and on toward a pale blue horizon.

Leaning on the metal railing, Janie spotted a small brown bird swooping low above the waves. Was it searching for food? The only birds she knew about lived in trees and ate worms. There was not a tree or a night crawler for hundreds of miles.

Just off the side of the boat, a long dark shadow rippled beneath the surface of the waves. Janie moved forward, following it. The creature's broad shiny back looked like a hippo's when it broke the water. It disappeared quickly. Janie leaned over the railing, trying to catch another glimpse.

"Careful there, Janie!"

She looked around.

"Up here!"

On the small overhanging deck Captain Bob, Steve, and Pete stood outside the wheelhouse.

"I just saw something."

"Watch for blasts of mist," Pete called. "That's whale's breath. We call it a blow."

"You mean it might have been a whale?" Nothing

in all her books had prepared her for the sight of that mammoth creature's shiny black skin.

"Probably."

With her hands sheltering her eyes, Janie scanned the water. The bright morning sun glinted on the waves. She waited.

"Janie!" Steve shouted. "Starboard." He pointed to the right.

"Oh, wow!" The last of a whale's white tail flukes sank beneath the waters.

"Ten o'clock!" Pete roared.

"What?" said Janie.

"The bow is twelve o'clock," the captain called. "Look toward where ten would be."

Janie turned. Off in the distance, misty jets shot up from the surface of the water. Whales' breath like geysers, one, then another, then two off by themselves, exploded all around the bow of the boat. It was like being at the center of a circus.

The boat's engines revved up, and the ship plowed through the waves toward the blows. "Good morning!" The captain's voice boomed over the loudspeaker. "It's five-twenty A.M. and we've got whales."

In minutes, the deck was crowded with sleepy-looking people, some still in pajamas with windbreakers on. Though half dressed, most had cameras.

Several, including Janie's father, had two slung around their necks.

"Dad, Dad." Janie worked her way through the crowd. "They're out there."

He gave her a hug. "You're up early."

"I couldn't sleep. Oh—" she said, "I should wake Courtney."

Just then on the other side of the deck, a short, white-haired woman called, "Over here, over here."

Everyone gathered at the railing. A few yards off and just beneath the water's surface, two massive gray bodies swam by.

Cameras clicked and whirred. Over the loudspeaker, Pete bellowed. "Sperm whales. I'd say Mom's about thirty-five feet long and the calf's twelve. Our boat's one hundred feet, so that will give you a sense of how big they are."

As the whales slipped away, two blows erupted in unison. Streaks of yellow, blue, and pink mist sparkled in the sunlight. Oohs and aahs came from all around the deck, interrupted by the captain's voice on the loudspeaker.

The captain said, "'His vast, mild head . . . glorified by a rainbow, as if Heaven itself has put its seal upon his thoughts.'"

Janie's father lowered his camera. "What a way to start the day—quoting Melville!"

"That's from *Moby Dick*," the captain said. "Not me."

"You should read that," Mr. Tannenbaum said.

Janie leaned on the railing. "I'll tell Harold. We could try it on the cows."

The *Yankee* navigated toward the blows. But as suddenly as the whales had appeared, they vanished beneath the waves.

Janie and her father stayed at the railing. "Dad, I can't get over the size of them. I mean they're bigger than dinosaurs!"

"And sperm whales aren't the biggest. The blues get to be one hundred feet."

"The length of this entire boat!" Janie tried to imagine one coming out of the water next to them.

"Well," Captain Bob said over the loudspeaker. "Looks like the whales have gone for breakfast. I guess we should too."

"But before you go," Pete said, "I'd like to mention that there will be a T-shirt for the person who correctly identifies the first of any species we see."

"Oh, man," Janie said. "I want to do that."

"Me too," said her father. "Well, I'll see you at breakfast. I want to make sure your mother's up."

The smells of bacon and coffee lured Janie into the

galley. She leaned against the door to the head across the galley passageway, hoping no one could hear her growling stomach. Ralph dished out eggs. Monica toasted bread.

Janie felt the door being pushed open. "Oops, sorry," she said stepping away.

"Oh! Hi, Janie." It was Courtney. "What was all the shouting about?"

"Sperm whales!"

"Really!"

"We saw a mother and baby. They were huge!"

"You should have called me."

"It happened so fast."

"I don't want to miss anything. Wake me when you get up tomorrow, okay?"

"Sure." Janie noticed Courtney's lavender sweater and matching slacks. She looked so pretty; she even had on purple jewelry.

Janie glanced down at her rumpled sweatshirt. It had catsup on it from last night's supper.

"Did you see Steve, Janie?"

"Yeah, on the upper deck. I guess I should go change."

"Breakfast!" Ralph called out.

"Come and get it before it runs away," Monica yelled.

"Forget it!" Janie laughed. "I'm starving."

After breakfast, people lingered in the dining area sipping coffee and chatting. Ralph cleaned the galley. Monica worked her way down the room wiping off tables.

Courtney looked around. "I wonder where he is?"

Janie said, "What are you up to?"

Courtney half smiled. "Let's go outside. It's too crowded in here."

The deserted back end of the boat was flooded with bright morning sunlight. The *Yankee*'s engines churned the water into foam as the boat chugged across the Gulf of Maine.

Janie sat on a narrow bench. Vibrations from the engine ran up her legs and into her stomach.

Courtney zipped her jacket and sat next to Janie. "I want to find out about Steve."

"Why—do you like him?"

"I have to figure out if he likes me, first."

"Is that how it works?"

"Janie!" Courtney laughed. "Don't you know anything about anything?"

"I don't know what I know."

"Well, just watch, then you can learn."

"I'm not sure I want to."

"Your attention, please!" Pete's voice boomed over the speaker system.

The *Yankee*'s engines suddenly cut back to an idle. With the motor's rumbling gone, the sound of sloshing water filled the air. The boat drifted peacefully.

"May I have everyone's attention, please. I have an important announcement."

Janie stood and leaned over the railing. Maybe another whale was out there. She didn't see any blows.

"We've just had a radio communiqué from a patrol boat," Pete began. "A whale has been sighted dragging a one hundred-foot fishing net. If you think you see something unusual, please let us know immediately. That's all for now."

Courtney put her hands in her pockets. "I wonder how that could happen?"

"Let's head up to the bow," Janie said.

They joined Janie's parents at the front of the boat. Pete stood on the upper deck with binoculars. "The nets are put out by the fishermen," he was saying, "to trap large schools of cod."

"Monsieur Pete," a man with a French accent called out, "how could the whale be entangled?"

"The nets are weighted to the seafloor by anchors.

The tops of the nets have buoys to keep them afloat, so they look like underwater tennis nets. Whales run right into them when they're chasing after fish."

"And the whale, it can be freed?"

"We don't have the equipment. But the patrol boat does. If it gets to the whale in time."

Janie looked at her mother. "What does he mean 'in time'?"

"Ask."

"What's 'in time,' Pete?"

Pete scratched his bearded chin. "Well, sometimes the whale can free itself, but often it'll just get even more wrapped up. If the net goes over its mouth and the whale's unable to feed, it dies of starvation."

People were quiet. The *Yankee* started up again.

"Mom, is this the kind of endangered animal stuff you'll be filming?"

"Yes, in part."

"I thought you'd just be having fun."

"Janie," said her father, "it's about how animals live and raise their young too. Not just dying."

"Starboard bow," the captain bellowed. "Dolphins coming in for a look at us."

The squeaking and clicking sounds of hundreds of dolphins caused everyone to turn. The dolphins had dark backs, long graceful lines of white and yellow on their sides, and pure white bellies. They leaped around the *Yankee,* jumping and tumbling over one another like eager puppies.

Courtney laughed. "Aren't they cute!"

"Yeah, look at those guys."

Several dolphins were racing along at the tip of the bowsprit. They seemed to be trying to point the boat in the direction they wanted it to head.

Janie said, "It's like Mr. Ransom's dogs herding the cows back to the barn. Harold would love it."

"It's called bowriding, Janie. Dolphins do the same thing to whales." Steve was right behind them.

"Hi, Steve!" Courtney's voice rose.

From the upper deck, Pete said, "Very often when we see dolphins, it means that whales are nearby. White-sided dolphins feed on the same schools of fish that whales sometimes like. They'll probably be along soon."

The dolphins played around the boat while people took pictures. Then as if by agreement, the dolphins headed off in another direction. The *Yankee* was alone again in a vast watery wilderness.

"See ya." Steve headed toward the galley.

"Well," said Pete after a while. "I guess the whales are a no-show, but then this isn't one of those amusement parks where the animals are trained to do tricks. We never know what to expect out here."

Janie stared off into the distance. Somewhere she'd heard about swimming with dolphins. You could climb on their backs and go for a ride.

"Janie, I'm just dying to talk to Steve. You have to help me figure out how."

"What did you say?"

CHAPTER 6

THE *Yankee* continued to plow across the churning Gulf of Maine. Some whale watchers stayed at the rail throughout the afternoon keeping track of the number of whales that were sighted. Another group counted birds, and a few people snoozed in the sun on the top deck.

After dinner, as the sinking sun cast a golden path across the pewter sea, Janie and Courtney came out on deck. Janie leaned on the rail. "What's going on, Dad?"

"Right now just seabirds feeding." Tiny blackish birds swirled silently above the water.

Vicky said, "Those sooty birds you see are pelagic and spend most of their lives at sea. They only return to land if the weather is very stormy or when it's time to breed."

"Gosh," Courtney said. "Can you imagine spending your life out here? It's so lonely."

"Maybe not to them," Janie said.

"Sailors," Vicky continued, "once called shearwaters the 'moaning birds' because the only sounds they make are on their breeding grounds, where they squeal around their nests. We'll probably see other seabirds like petrels and phalaropes while—"

"Look!" Janie said.

Near the middle of the boat, a whale's head broke through the water, lunging straight up into the air. The solid black form cut the sinking sun in half before it fell back into the water.

"There's another one," Janie cried.

Some people started for the bow. "Come on, Courtney," said Janie. "I want to find out what those whales are doing."

Three other whales with opened mouths came up out of the ocean in unison. Water cascaded down their sides.

"Janie, let's ask Steve. I see him up there."

"Okay." Janie walked forward watching for whales.

Near the bow, Courtney squeezed in at the railing. "Hi, Steve."

"Hi," he said, concentrating on the water.

Janie stood behind them. She peered between their shoulders.

Courtney smiled. "Steve, what's going on?"

He pointed. "See that circle floating on top of the water. That's a bubble cloud. The whales blow bubbles right beneath the surface of the water to trap their food. Now watch that spot."

Sure enough. There was a smooth round place that looked like a giant contact lens resting on the grayish waves. All of a sudden, right up through the center of the circle, the whale's head rose. Bumpy knobs like big black grapefruits dotted its head and jaws.

"Humpback! Humpback!" Janie cried.

"T-shirt!" Steve shouted. "For the girl with red hair!"

Everyone laughed and clapped. Janie grinned.

Courtney leaned closer. "I wish I'd known that."

"Next one," Janie whispered. "I'll tell you."

"Over there!" An older woman pointed.

Another whale rose out of the water. Pete said, "That was about a one-hundred pound mouthful. As the whale forces the water out of its mouth, some food falls back into the ocean. That's what the birds are counting on. I've seen a few almost become whale supper that way."

They watched until it grew dark. When a gusty wind began blowing, everyone headed indoors.

"Bye, Steve," Courtney called. He waved over his shoulder, heading aft.

"Janie, he never says anything to me unless I ask a question."

"Maybe he's shy."

"Why would he be? It doesn't make sense."

Janie shrugged. "Let's go inside."

In the dining area, Mrs. Tannenbaum sat poring over an album on her lap. "Look at these photographs," she said. "They're gorgeous."

One picture showed three people stretched over the side of a blown-up rubber boat petting a whale. "Oh, man! wouldn't you love to be them?" said Janie.

Courtney made a face. "I can't believe they get so close."

Mrs. Tannenbaum turned the page. "Pete and Vicky talked about doing it. I bet it'd be fun."

The door near the galley slid open. Janie's father stepped inside. "Janie, you and Courtney should head out to the stern. Pete and Steve are hauling in fish like crazy. It's really something to see."

Janie smiled at Courtney. "Want to?"

Courtney nodded eagerly.

"See you later, guys."

Janie slid open the stern passageway. Moonlight fell on the silver fish that lay flapping on the deck.

"Eee," said Courtney stepping over them.

"Jeez. They're as big as Fang."

Pete cast his rod. "Who's Fang?"

"My killer poodle."

Steve laughed. "You want to try fishing?"

"Absolutely," said Janie.

"I'll watch," Courtney said.

"We've actually got enough," Pete said. "I don't think you should, Janie. I'd rather just take what we need for now."

Janie nodded. Harold would say something like that.

"Hey—" Steve reeled his last fish up out of the water and pulled it into the boat. "Look at that sucker."

"Nice," said Pete.

"A beauty," said Janie.

Steve's large chapped hand probed inside the fish's mouth. With one yank, he pulled out the hook.

Courtney looked away. Oh, poor fish, Janie thought, if only Harold could have done that.

The cod lay on the deck with its bloody mouth opening and closing. Its tail flapped against another fish. The eye grew filmy.

Steve set aside his pole and pulled a knife from a leather holder on his belt. He pressed the knife into the fish at the tail end and slid it all the way up the stomach toward the head. Water spilled out.

Janie thought of Harold's long, slender fingers. His thumbnail had a deep crease. It was the thumb that tried to stroke the fish's belly.

"Guts overboard." Steve tossed the innards into the water. Fishblood trickled down his thumb. "You want to see inside the stomach? It's pretty neat."

"Janie," Courtney whispered. "I have to get out of here. Bye," she said aloud. "See you tomorrow."

Steve tossed the fillets into a bucket of water. "I don't blame you. It's gross."

"Bye," said Janie. Too bad Courtney didn't stay. Steve was okay. "I'd like to see what's inside."

Steve gutted another fish. He poked the knife into the stomach sack. "See the krill?" The knife tip probed at a pink shrimplike creature.

Janie studied it. "Glad that isn't my supper."

"Actually," said Pete, "krill're good, like crab. And krill're eaten by cod and cod by us. These'll be tomorrow's meal."

"Hey—the food chain!" Janie said.

"Absolutely," Pete continued. "There've been times when I've seen so much krill floating in the ocean it looked like tomato soup."

Janie laughed. That was one to tell Harold.

"Then there's this." Steve took a metal ring from a soda can out of the stomach.

Pete shook his head. "I hate it."

"Me too." Janie said.

"Me three." Steve tossed it into a garbage pail roped to the wall.

"Attention, please," the captain's voice came over the loudspeaker. "I'd like every crew member to report to the bridge in fifteen minutes."

Steve looked up. "Wonder what's going on?"

"I'll finish gutting," Pete said. "Steve, you start hosing down the deck."

"Can I help?" Janie asked.

"No, but thanks," Pete said.

"I'd like to, if you ever need it."

Janie pulled open the curtain to her cabin. "Hi, there."

"Oh," groaned Courtney. "Did I ever blow that one. Steve probably thinks I'm a wimp."

"No, he doesn't." Janie flopped down on Courtney's bunk, next to her.

"Did he say anything about me after I left?"

"No. We just looked at fish guts."

Courtney shook her head. "I'm glad I missed it."

"Your attention, again," came the captain's voice. "Sorry to keep interrupting. I've set up a special watch for that entangled whale. We'll keep floodlights on till just before dawn. Steve will be lookout for the next two hours, followed by Vicky, then Pete, then Steve again. You're welcome to join them."

"Courtney!"

"What?"

"Go look for that whale with him."

"Me?"

"Yes. It's a little cold, but at least he won't be gutting fish."

"Janie, you're brilliant!"

Janie laughed. "Oh, it's true."

"Janie, you do know more about this boy stuff than you think."

"I'm trying real hard not to."

"Well, I just don't want Steve to think I'm a baby. I mean, I'm really not, Janie."

"I know. I was in the hospital with you."

Courtney picked up her brush. "I better fix my hair."

"Quit worrying; get up there."

Courtney's lilac perfume lingered in the air after she left. Janie climbed up on the top bunk and stretched out on her stomach. She opened her whale book.

Steve really was nice. He would be super for Courtney after that creepy guy Mark.

He was decent, except for the way he tore out a

fishhook. Once Harold said that the Indians used to ask forgiveness from a fish before they killed it. Respect for what they killed, Harold had said.

Janie studied the photographs. Men in old-fashioned clothes stood, harpoons in hand, beside a dead whale. She groaned and turned the page. The ocean waves along the shoreline were red from the blood of a butchered whale. "Oh, gross."

The curtain snapped open. "I give up!" Courtney swept in and flopped on her cot.

Janie closed the book. "What happened?" She leaned over the edge of her bunk to talk.

"I don't get it, Janie. I know I'm not that ugly. What's his problem?"

"Ugly! What'd you mean?"

"All he talks about is whales, whales, whales."

"You're exaggerating."

"No, I'm not. I asked him about dances at his school, and he mumbled something about Monica. I guess they live in the same town."

"Huh. Well, maybe he thinks you're too young."

"No. I told him we were in tenth."

"Yikes! Me too?"

Courtney sat up on her cot. She and Janie were almost nose to nose. "I think maybe you're more his type."

"What?" said Janie.

"Really! Whales, the outdoors . . . fish guts."

"No, way! You're the one who likes him. Not me."

Courtney threw up her hands. "I don't know anything about whales, and he smells of fish."

Janie hooted. "Well, yeah. He was gutting them."

"See—more your type. Even if Mark was a jerk, at least we talked about movies. Janie, you should get to know Steve, not me."

Janie pushed herself back up on her bed. "I have to go to sleep. Good night."

CHAPTER 7

"RISE and shine," Janie said the next morning. "It's time." Janie shook Courtney's shoulder. "You said you wanted me to wake you early."

Courtney rolled away toward the wall. "What time is it?" she groaned.

"Morning time!" Janie shook her again.

"Oh, Janie please. I don't feel good."

"What's wrong?"

"I don't know. My stomach's upset."

"You want me to get my mother?"

"No, I just need to sleep some more."

"You sure?"

Courtney pulled the blankets up to her shoulder and snuggled down. "I'll be okay."

It would probably be a good idea, Janie thought, if she found her mother anyway. She climbed the ladder.

The sky was overcast. The deck was wet. Must have rained. She looked around for her parents.

Steve walked toward her. Dressed in a yellow rain slicker and slicker overalls, he looked exactly like the fisherman on the frozen fish boxes.

"'Morning, Janie."

His face was covered with little dots of rain. One drop slid down his nose and dripped onto his jacket. She liked the smell of fish and salt coming from him. "Hi," she said. "Just getting off watch?"

Steve pushed his hood off. "Yup." He unzipped the slicker. Underneath he wore the T-shirt with the two whales.

"Did you see any signs of that entangled whale?"

"Nothing."

"Too bad. Hey, can I get a shirt like yours?"

Steve looked down. "You mean this cow and calf duo?"

"Is that what they are?"

"You know what the male's called?"

"A bull?"

"Yup."

"Just like the cows at home."

"You have cows?" He slid the jacket off his shoulder.

"I don't, but the farmer up the road does. I milk. My friend Harold reads to keep them calm."

"I'll have to tell my aunt. She has a farm in Wisconsin."

Steve talked about stuff other than whales, Janie thought. Courtney was wrong.

"Want to see something interesting?" He reached into his pocket.

Janie studied the pointed white object in Steve's open hand. "Looks like a tooth," she said.

"It's a porpoise tooth."

Janie picked it up. The hard smooth surface looked as if it had been polished.

"Porpoises are really whales," Steve said, "but they have teeth."

"I didn't know that." Janie glanced up. He had the palest blue eyes. She hadn't noticed that before.

"Janie, are you coming to tomorrow's lecture?"

"What? Oh, sure."

"They'll be talking about odontoceti, which are toothed whales, and mysticeti, the baleen whales."

Janie nodded, trying to pay attention.

"You can have that tooth. Pete gave me a couple, but bring it to the talk, so we can show everyone."

"Hey—thanks! I will."

"Steve!" Monica came toward them. "I've been waiting for you in the galley."

Steve looked at his watch. "I better get going."

"Wait—" said Janie. "Have you seen my parents?"

"They're up in my father's quarters."

"How do I get up there?"

"You can't."

"Why not?"

"No one's allowed."

"This is important. Courtney's sick."

"Oh," he said.

"Steve!" Monica walked closer. "You promised you'd help me set up."

"I'll get a message to your parents, Janie." He hurried after Monica.

"Thanks," Janie called. He really was okay.

Moments later, Janie opened the curtain. Courtney was dressed but sitting on her cot. "You feeling any better?"

"A little." Courtney fingered the pierced earrings in her hand.

"You know what? I was just talking to Steve. Look at this tooth he said I could have."

"He gave you one of his teeth?"

Janie laughed. "No, it's from a porpoise."

"See, Janie. Your type." Courtney tried to find the hole in her earlobe with the earring post.

"Courtney! He was just being nice."

Courtney couldn't get her earrings on. She tossed them into her suitcase and stood slowly. There was sweat on her upper lip.

"Did you take any seasickness stuff?"

"I can't find it."

"You checked everywhere?"

Courtney let out a low moan. She bent over, holding her stomach.

"What's wrong?"

"I'm going to throw up."

"Quick," said Janie. "Up on deck."

Janie hurried Courtney into the passageway. They had to wait for Ralph to climb the ladder ahead of them.

"Hang on, Courtney," Janie said as they started up. "We're almost there."

In the dining room, Janie slid the door partway open and propped Courtney against it. "Take deep breaths."

Janie took deep breaths too. The air felt delicious and cool on her face after the closeness of the cabin below.

Outside, foam sprayed up against the starboard

deck as the *Yankee* plunged through choppy seas. Janie concentrated on the gray sky.

"Ja-nie!" Courtney wailed. "Everything's rocking up and down."

"Look at your hands, not the horizon. Think about anything but getting sick."

"Like what?"

"What's the happiest thing you can think of?"

"Dying!"

Just then Janie saw her father coming into the galley. "Dad! Courtney's seasick."

"We were just coming to find you."

The minute Mrs. Tannenbaum saw Courtney, she said, "Oh, I feel terrible. I picked up your medication from the backseat of the car when we were unloading. I put it with ours and forgot all about it."

Janie's mother placed a small sticker behind Courtney's ear. "Don't take this off, and you'll be fine."

"Thanks, Mrs. Tannenbaum. I think I'll go lie down again."

Janie's father said, "Let the patch get working before you go below. Most likely, it'll make you drowsy, then you can catch forty winks."

"Okay," said Courtney.

"Let's go out on deck," Janie's mother said. "The air will help."

They all headed toward the bow. Courtney sat on a bench and closed her eyes. Janie and her parents joined a crowd, some with binoculars and others with cameras, all waiting for something to happen.

At the railing was one of the Japanese men. Not much taller than Janie, he had short black hair and glasses. *"Nagasu kujira! Nagasu kujira!"* He pointed.

"What's wrong?" Janie said.

"I'm not sure," said her father.

"Fin whale, three o'clock!" Pete's voice boomed.

A long sleek body cut through the choppy waters. A glimpse of the grayish white streak on its side was possible before it disappeared.

"Way to go," Janie cheered. Other people clapped.

"Fin whales are one of the least understood whales," Pete said. "They're smaller than the blue whales but better built for speed. I think Mr. Kimura should get a T-shirt not only for spotting the first fin but for also giving us the Japanese translation."

Everyone applauded. Mr. Kimura bowed his head slightly.

Janie pronounced it slowly. *"Na-ga-su ku-jira?"*

Mr. Kimura nodded.

A woman on the other side of the bow shouted, "How long are they?"

Steve yelled, "Up to eighty feet—your basic school bus."

Janie chuckled. He was pretty funny.

"Janie, look!" Mrs. Tannenbaum adjusted the camera lens and began photographing.

"Holy cow," Pete bellowed over the speaker. "Blue whale! Port bow. Behold, the largest mammal that ever lived!"

Janie grabbed for the railing as people crowded around. Cameras whirred and clicked. The whale's grayish blue back went on forever. "Jeez," Janie said. "It's an island swimming by."

"I can't believe it," said her mother.

Pete said, "That blue's a first for me. We've had reports of blues up here, but even the rumors are rare."

"*Nagasu kujira?*" Janie pointed to where the blue had vanished.

Mr. Kimura shook his head. "*Shiro nagasu kujira* is the blue whale."

"*Shiro nagasu kujira,*" she said slowly. "Boy, will Harold be impressed!'

It rained all that afternoon, making sightings more difficult. In the dining room, some people watched a video about whales. Others slept in their cabins or read whale books Pete and Vicky had brought along. By late in the day only a few more whale sightings had been noted in the whale-watchers' log.

After dinner that night, Courtney and Janie went out on deck. The sky was still overcast and the sea covered with white caps, but the wind had died down.

"How you doing?" Janie asked.

"The patch is making me sleepy, but I don't want to give in and go to bed."

Janie nodded. "Yeah, it's pretty early still."

Vicky stood at the rail with Janie's parents. "Hi," she said. "Come join us. We're watching for—"

"What is that?" Mr. Tannenbaum pointed to the water.

Thirty to forty fins sliced through the waves, coming steadily toward the boat.

"Are those what I think they are?" Mrs. Tannenbaum asked.

"If you're thinking sharks," said Vicky, "you're right. They're basking sharks."

"*Dun,* dun dun dun. *Dun,* dun, dun, dun." Steve sang coming up behind them. He was carrying a sack of potatoes.

Janie burst out laughing. He was humming the theme from that old shark movie, *Jaws.*

"Back to the galley, Steve!" Vicky laughed.

Courtney stared at the water. Her face was ashen.

Green mottled sharks broke into clusters of fours and fives inspecting the *Yankee*'s hull. They were slow moving but, Janie thought, the swaying fins were really creepy.

"They're so big." Janie's mother took several photographs.

"About thirty feet long," Vicky said. "But nothing to be afraid of. Sharks are really not menacing creatures."

"Oh, sure!" said Courtney.

"No, really," Vicky insisted. "These basking sharks only eat plankton, tiny organisms that float on the currents. You could go swimming with this crew."

Janie slapped the railing. "Boy, wouldn't that be something to tell your friends."

Courtney frowned. "You'd do it?"

"You bet!"

Courtney shook her head. "I'm such a coward."

"No, you're not."

"I sure feel like one."

In a few moments the sharks disappeared. "Well," said Vicky, "those seabirds you see over there—"

"Your attention once again," the captain said.

"We've just had another report about that entangled whale. It's traveling in this direction. If you see anything, let us know."

"Boy," said Janie. "I hope it doesn't come into contact with any sharks. Even if those basking sharks won't hurt it, some others might."

"I'm going in." Courtney said.

CHAPTER 8

JANIE opened her eyes and yawned. She stretched peacefully. All around her was the low steady hum of the *Yankee's* engines and the sounds of water.

It didn't feel like morning, but she had to use the bathroom. The head, she reminded herself.

A cool, salty breeze greeted her but no daylight as she made her way up the ladder and through the dining area. The ship's clock said 4:30 A.M. Still the middle of the night, but she was wide-awake.

The door to the head was latched open to keep it from swinging. Janie undid the hook and stepped over the high sill.

The boat's listing was so gentle that balancing on the toilet was no challenge. But, Janie thought, it had to be tricky to stay on the seat in a storm.

The salt water Janie splashed in her face made her

skin tingle. She stuck her tongue out at the mirror, then relatched the door in the open position.

Maybe she should get Courtney up. But that wasn't really fair.

She wandered into the galley and opened the double-door refrigerator. Steve's bucket of fish sat next to a plate of brownies covered in plastic wrap. A huge bag of carrots rested on a gallon of milk.

Hmm, thought Janie. A raid! Just like home. She took a brownie and a cup of milk and went to stand at the stern end of the boat.

With zillions of stars visible, the sky had a different feel. It looked dusty. She knew all about the constellations because Harold had been the one who pointed them out when they were little kids.

Janie munched and searched for the Big Dipper with its long handle. It was there, same as ever. She found the Little Dipper next and Cassiopeia's Chair after that. Harold would have loved this trip.

Twangy music like something from an old sailor movie floated down the deck. Janie popped the last of the brownie into her mouth and dropped the empty cup in a barrel roped to the wall.

She walked forward. A figure dressed in a poncho leaned against the rail, playing a harmonica.

The melody circled and spun. She stepped up onto the bowsprit. "Steve?"

"Janie?"

"Yeah, what are you doing?"

"I'm hoping that entangled whale will come and listen."

"Can I watch with you?"

"Sure."

The narrow bowsprit, jutting from the bow, was like a long walkway enclosed with railing. Steve pressed himself against the rail on one side. Janie slid along the other rail trying to get past him. Their bodies brushed against each other.

"Oh," she said glancing up. Steve smiled at her.

Janie faced the ocean, glad that he couldn't see she'd gone red. The wind blew cooling mist against her cheeks. She licked her lips, tasting salt and chocolate.

Steve played. Harmonica music danced over her shoulder into the night.

The boat motored quietly. On and on it went. When Steve stopped playing, he placed his hands on both sides of the bowsprit railing. His arm resting against Janie's felt warm. She didn't move away.

Steve said almost in her ear, "I met a guy who said he'd heard whales snoring."

"No!"

Steve laughed. "Through the blowholes on their backs."

"Oh, that's so neat."

"Yeah. He said when you touch a whale, the skin's so sensitive, the entire body trembles."

"Really," said Janie. "What's it feel like?"

"Amazingly soft. Janie, look!"

Over at the rim of the ocean, a thin ray of light stretched out along the horizon. The streak reached upward too, turning the low-lying clouds pink.

Janie had never seen anything like it. She felt her eyes gobbling up the shape of the earth.

"Listen," he said. There was a long watery sigh. "A whale holds its breath down to the bottom of the ocean and then comes up."

She heard the sigh again. It was the wind from another world.

They could barely see the whale turned on its side. It was swimming along keeping up with the boat.

"Steve, he's looking right at us!"

"He's checking us out."

Janie hung over the railing. "Hi, there."

"His eye looks like ours, doesn't it?"

"I know. I can't believe it. But it's not the entangled one, is it?"

"I don't think so; I don't see any fishnet, which is kind of like the mesh bags onions come in."

The whale's huge white flipper began slapping the ocean. Each time he lowered the mighty winglike flipper, water sprang up at them.

"Woa!" Janie roared. This was the best shower she'd ever had.

Steve leaned closer to Janie. His chest pressed against her shoulder. Hot shivers ran up her spine. She gripped the bowsprit railings and slowly leaned back against him.

The whale disappeared beneath the surface of the water. "Where's he going?"

Steve bent over the railing again. "I bet he'll be back."

Darn, Janie thought. If she hadn't said anything, Steve wouldn't have moved.

With daylight breaking to the east, the sleek black body and white flippers lunged straight out of the ocean. Up and up hurled the thirty tons, then over onto its side, and for an instant, the entire body was out of the water.

"Jump again!" she shouted as the enormous whale plunged into the water. Salt water drenched Janie to the bone.

"What a show he's putting on for you. That's breaching."

Janie pressed against the starboard rail, waiting and

watching. All was quiet. She shivered from the wind blowing against her.

"You should go in," Steve said. "You don't have on a jacket."

"Not a chance. I wouldn't miss this."

A bank of dark clouds rolled along the horizon. The wind picked up. The seas and winds swirled around the *Yankee.*

Janie shivered again.

"Sure you don't want to go below?"

"No way!"

Steve put his arm around her shoulders, enfolding her in his woolen poncho. She wrapped her arms around his waist and snuggled against him for warmth. Oh, it felt so good!

An enormous black-and-white whale's tail rose up right next to the bowsprit. The fifteen-foot flukes were so close, Janie could see scars and gashes. The sea splashed over the bowsprit like a waterfall.

Steve hung on to her as the boat pitched, then righted itself. Foam rolled down the deck and over the sides. The whale slipped beneath the ocean.

Coughing on salt water, Steve said, "You all right?"

"Yeah." She shook water out of her ears.

"You weren't scared at all, were you?"

"No way!"

"The girls I know would've been! You're terrific, Janie Tannenbaum." He put both arms around Janie and hugged her. She hugged him back.

Janie wrapped her arms around her legs and leaned back against the cabin wall. Water squished out of her socks when she curled up her toes. Courtney sat on the bunk, still in pajamas. "So, what happened with you and Steve, Janie?"

"Today," the loudspeaker interrupted, "we'll be traveling along the Browns Bank where right whales have been sighted at this time of year. Don't miss Vicky and Pete's lecture."

"I forgot about that." Janie hoisted herself off the floor. She needed to put on dry clothing.

"Janie, you have to tell me everything. Remember how we promised?"

Janie peeled off her soaked sweatshirt. "You sure you don't feel bad that I was hanging around with him?"

Courtney rummaged in her suitcase. "I think it's great."

"But what about you? I thought you liked him."

"He smelled of fish. Remember?"

"Yeah, but—"

"But, nothing. I never thought about this before,

but I like movies and bus fumes, not fishy guys. Besides, you finally like a boy."

"Well, I don't know if I'd go that far."

"Oh, come on!"

"Okay. Okay. Maybe, just a little." She could make those hot shivers run down her back again if she thought about Steve hugging her.

"You think you'll meet him up there again?"

"I don't know."

"Did he kiss you, Janie?"

"No way! Are you ready for breakfast?"

"I'll see you up there, Janie. Save me a seat. I want to see what's going to happen with you and Steve."

"Get out," Janie said, but she left before Courtney noticed she was blushing.

CHAPTER 9

AFTER breakfast, Pete picked up the microphone in the dining room. "We'll start our lecture in ten minutes."

Steve, Vicky, and Pete set up the slide projector and screen while people chatted. "Okay!" Pete called, "We're all organized." Everyone settled down.

Janie slid into the first booth. Courtney sat beside her.

"Since it's gotten so overcast out there," Pete began, "I think you'll be able to see the slides just fine. Vicky has a few things to say first."

Vicky moved into the center aisle. "Whales, dolphins, and porpoises are sea mammals. Just like us, they're warm-blooded, breathe air, and suckle their young. They're called cetaceans and are divided into two groups. Those with teeth and those with baleen."

Steve leaned over and said something to Pete. "Excuse me," Pete interrupted. "We have a sample from a toothed whale, better known as a porpoise. Okay Janie, it's time to be the tooth fairy."

Courtney kicked Janie under the table. Janie kicked back. She didn't dare look at Steve.

Janie fished the tooth out of her pocket and stood up. "Odontoceti," she said passing the tooth to the Kimuras in the next booth.

"Very good!" Pete said.

Janie glanced at her father. He winked. Her mother smiled.

Vicky continued. "The baleen, which replaces teeth in certain kinds of whales, hangs down from the upper jaw like vertical blinds you might put on your windows at home. Starting from one side of the mouth, baleen makes a horseshoe shape around to the other side of the jaw. The baleen plates are hard like our fingernails and help the animals to strain fish and plankton from water. Baleen can be up to twelve feet long."

Vicky handed Janie a hunk of baleen. It looked like a piece of a gigantic comb. Janie passed it along to Courtney saying, "Poor whale."

Courtney grimaced. Gingerly, she looked it over and passed it on.

Vicky said, "Let's see the slides."

The first picture flashed on the screen. "Here's a right whale with his snout out of the water."

In the close-up photo, Janie saw baleen hanging from the whale's jaw. "Think how big that mouth is," she said.

"The baleen looks like fringe," Courtney said.

Pete stepped in front of the screen. He reached out a hand as if to stroke the top of the whale's head. "Early whalers called this creature a right whale because it was 'right' to kill. It swam close to shore and moved slowly, so it was easy to harpoon. It floated when dead and yielded huge amounts of oil. There were thousands upon thousands once, but now they're close to extinction."

"How awful," Courtney whispered.

Someone at the back of the room said, "Does anyone know how many are left?"

"We don't," Pete said. "Scientists think about three hundred, but we're not certain if the numbers are increasing or decreasing. We're seeing more right whales now, but it's because we're looking in places we've never looked before. Over the last few years, Browns Bank is where right whales have been sighted doing their wooing."

Pete moved out of the way of the screen. The snout of another whale appeared.

"Notice," Vicky pointed, "the big white spots on

the head. Those patches are one way to identify—"

"Hey, Pete—" Steve pointed out the window.

Outside the gray water was foaming and churning. V-shaped puffs of mist spouted one after another.

Over the loudspeaker, came the captain's voice. "Right whales, three o'clock."

"Okay!" Pete laughed. "Class is over. On deck for a visit with the rarest of whales. With any luck, we'll catch some flirtation—whale-style."

Janie, Steve, and Pete were the first to reach the starboard rail. Courtney and Vicky came up behind.

The waves slapped at the boat. Flippers and flukes broke the water at all different angles as the whales sighed and thrashed. It was hard to tell where one whale began and another ended.

"What is going on?" Janie shouted.

Vicky laughed. "We call it courting behavior."

"What?" said Courtney.

"The two strongest males work to position themselves on either side of the female. The weaker ones jockey around on the edges, but they don't stand a chance."

"Sounds like the dances at school," Steve said.

Janie hooted. Steve smiled at her.

Courtney glanced at Steve, then Janie.

The sea foamed like a boiling soup. One whale

lifted its flukes, preparing to dive. Another plowed along the surface of the waves spouting mist.

"The female's gone belly-up!" Vicky shouted. "Look at the white blaze."

The waves mostly covered the whale, but Janie caught a flash of the pure white belly. The white was so startling against the black, it looked painted on.

"Why'd she do that?" Janie asked.

"Some scientists," said Pete, "think the female gets tired of being approached by the males so she makes it more difficult for them by rolling onto her back."

"Another theory," said Vicky, "is that it's a form of selection, because only the strongest, most agile male can mate with her."

Courtney said, "Maybe she's just playing hard to get."

"Whatever it is," Pete said, "I want it documented on video. There must be fifteen whales in that group. Come on, Steve."

"See you later," Steve called as they hurried away.

"Courtney, isn't this amazing?"

"I don't know. All that commotion out there looks pretty scary."

Vicky shook her head. "It may seem like all those males are ganging up on her, but there's neither aggression nor affection as we know it in what they're doing. These are animals, not kids at a dance. We try hard not to think or speak of them in human terms."

"Are they going to—well you know?" Janie said.

Vicky shrugged. "We know so little about right whales. Scientists aren't even sure if the courting behavior leads to the female getting pregnant."

Janie shook her head. "That's incredible."

"Maybe," said Courtney, "we'll see something that's never been seen before."

"It could happen." Vicky looked around. "Let's go topside. We'll get a better view from there."

"Great." Janie started up the ladder.

The sky was growing steadily darker, and the winds tore across the open deck. Janie, Courtney, and Vicky stood watching at the upper stern rail.

The backs of two black creatures surfaced. The waves broke over them, but they seemed perfectly comfortable.

"Your attention, please," the captain said. "Vicky report to the wheelhouse. Everyone else head inside."

"I have to find out what the captain wants. You two should go below."

"We will," Janie said, but she didn't move.

One whale rolled onto its side. It raised a paddle-like flipper and waved it idly in the air.

"Look at that!" Janie pointed.

"Janie, it's really getting dark," Courtney said.

"I want to see what's going to happen."

The whale's flipper flailed above the water. The other whale disappeared beneath the waves.

It started to rain. Large cold drops pelted Janie and Courtney.

"We should go, Janie."

"One more second."

The wind roared out of the north; the rain fell in sheets. All the seabirds were gone.

"I'm going," Courtney said.

"Okay. I'll be right there." Janie didn't move.

Great swells crashed over the whales and slammed into the boat. Heavy thick clouds crowded out the light.

For the second time that day, Janie was drenched to the bone. She couldn't have cared less.

"Attention," Captain Bob's voice crackled. "Everyone inside! I don't want anyone falling on a slippery deck."

Janie started down the ladder, but she stopped midway for one last look. The thick rain and sudden darkness made it difficult to see. Just as she was about to give up, the whales turned blaze to blaze, belly to belly. The two gigantic bodies rocked with the waves while their mighty flippers churned the sea into froth.

Janie danced around the doorway dripping water on the floor. "Oh, Courtney. You should have stayed."

"I couldn't. It was too rough." Courtney hung on to the edge of the cot. The boat was pitching and rolling.

"Are you okay?" said Janie.

"Yeah, now that I'm inside I am."

"I know Vicky wouldn't like this, but it was like those whales were actually hugging each other."

With a towel in her free hand, Courtney tried drying her hair. "Janie, when I came in, I overheard Steve asking where you were."

Janie leaned against the wall for balance. "What did he say?" She peeled off her wet slacks and let them fall in a heap.

" 'Where's Janie? She's not still out on deck, is she?' "

Janie reached for a dry sweater. "Who was he talking to?"

"Monica."

"Did you say they go to the same school?"

"I'm pretty sure. I bet he's falling in love with you."

Janie looked up from zipping her dry jeans. "Be real!"

"Is that what you're going to say if he asks you to meet him again?"

Janie cracked up laughing. "Knowing me. Probably. Boy, it's getting really rough."

"I'm trying to ignore it." Courtney pulled her hair back into an elastic band. She missed a large strand and shoved it behind her ear. "Really, Janie, what if he does?"

Janie shrugged. "Maybe, I'll just say no."

"You can't!"

Janie couldn't resist teasing. "I might."

"But—"

"Or maybe," Janie said slowly, "I'll ask him out."

"You wouldn't!"

"Why not?"

"Well, but—"

Janie threw back her head and laughed. "Okay, I'm all set. Are you ready?"

"I guess so. I'm a wreck, but I can't do anything the way the boat is rocking."

"Don't worry. You look great."

In the dining room, Steve stood bent over a small round table. He was hanging on to it, leafing through one of the photo albums.

"Steve," Janie said, "did you see the two whales at the stern?"

"Yes, we got some shots of them. I'm just trying to figure out who they were."

"How can you?" Courtney said, clinging to the table.

Steve kept the album from sliding off. "See the warty growths and patches on this whale's jaw, Scientists use them to identify each whale from year to year. They even name them."

"Oh, neat! What were the names of the pair we saw?"

"I'm not sure, Janie. I have some checking to do."

The photo album slid across the table as the *Yankee* pitched sharply to one side.

"Woa!" Janie grabbed for a table.

Courtney fell into a booth.

"Hang on," Steve said. "It's getting a little rough."

CHAPTER 10

THE storm grew steadily worse all day. The boat's seesawing made simple things like walking and reading or just sitting still quite difficult.

Some people stayed in their cabins, hoping to sleep. Others hung around in the galley in case they needed to use the head. Everyone, even the crew, was feeling queasy.

"Your attention, please," the captain said. "We'll be dining early tonight. We want to batten down the hatches before this gale gets any worse."

"Janie, I can't eat."

"Okay, keep me company. Grab a table."

Courtney slumped down in the closest booth. Janie worked her way forward grabbing on to tables and backs of booths. Vicky and Steve were in the dinner line with her parents.

"Cook looks green," Vicky said.

Steve lurched into the galley and leaned over the counter. "Want some help?"

Ralph nodded, thrusting the spatula at Steve. Without a word, he hurried out the stern passageway.

"Even Ralph's hair was greenish," Steve said, and moved behind the steam table next to Monica.

Janie's parents took their plates and staggered back down the aisle. "Are you both all right?" Mrs. Tannenbaum grabbed on to the back of a booth.

"Sure," Janie said. "This is great!"

Janie's father shook his head. The boat pitched to one side. He barely made it to a table.

Behind the counter, Monica placed a slice of bread on a plate each time Steve dished out a portion of fish. It was like a dance they did in time to the rocking of the boat.

"Steve, remember our first trip?" Monica said.

Steve eased a serving of fish onto a plate. "I still can't face carrot cake. That was the last thing I ate before the storm."

"All I remember is holding hands with you and barfing. Hi, Janie."

Steve glanced up. He frowned at Monica. "Want extra bread, Janie? It was made today."

Janie shook her head and took a plate.

"You getting seasick?"

"I'm all right." Janie's throat felt dry. She lumbered down the aisle, clutching for the edges of tables and backs of booths. Finally she made it to where Courtney was sitting. Janie fell into the seat and let go of her plate. It slid toward the window, then skidded back. She grabbed it.

"Courtney! Steve could be Monica's boyfriend. She just said something about holding hands with him and barfing."

"Oh, please!" Courtney rolled her eyes. "Don't mention that word."

"I know. All of a sudden, I don't feel so hot either."

Captain Bob suggested everyone retire early that night. There wasn't much else to do in a storm.

Down on the lower deck, the rolling and pitching of the boat made it impossible to just stand still in front of the sink. Janie and Courtney crashed into the wall and each other trying to wash before bed. They gave up on brushing their teeth. Even Courtney crawled into her cot fully dressed.

With the light turned out, they rocked in their bunks as each wave crashed against the bow. Some swells were so powerful, the boat shuddered as if it might crack open.

"I'm so nauseous," Courtney moaned. "That seasickness patch can't be working."

"I heard the captain say the storm had died down. It won't get any worse."

"Janie, I'd be lost without you."

"Same here."

They said good night, but the sounds of water slapping and gushing and falling kept Janie awake. With her eyes closed, she was reeling ten times worse than on the Whirlwind with Harold.

Janie opened her eyes. The ceiling, walls, and floor slid back where they belonged, but there was no getting away from the sounds of water bashing at the boat.

Janie closed her eyes, and the sick dizzy feeling started again. She sat up and threw off her covers. She couldn't stay below.

"Courtney?" Janie climbed down. Courtney was fast asleep. Wow! That was a surprise.

Janie dragged her sleeping bag off the bunk and up the ladder. The dining room lights were off except for one near the galley.

In the shadows, Ralph lay slumped over in a booth, his head resting on the table. He was snoring.

Vicky and Pete were stretched out in sleeping bags

on the floor at the bow end of the dining room. Janie couldn't tell who else was there.

With her sleeping bag wrapped around her, Janie climbed into a booth. She leaned her head against the window and eased her legs out. Across the aisle, Monica and Steve sat huddled under a blanket. Monica had her head on his shoulder. They were fast asleep.

Janie flung herself out of the booth. Outside the wind and waves railed against the boat, which suddenly felt very small in a vast, mean ocean.

She dropped her sleeping bag below deck and climbed down the ladder. All the lights were off in the cabins.

"Mom?" Janie called softly through the curtain. "Mom? Are you awake?"

She could just barely make out her mother in the lower bunk. Her father was asleep in the top one.

If only she could squeeze in with her mother, but the cots were too narrow. She dragged her sleeping bag back to her cabin.

In her own bunk again, Janie tossed and turned. Even covering her head with a pillow didn't drown out the sound of crashing water. The *Yankee*'s timbers groaned. There was no way she could fall asleep.

What seemed like a short time later, Janie heard

a shout in the storm. She turned. Men in old-fashioned clothing hurried down the deck of a three-masted whaler.

Up in the crow's nest, the lookout cried, "Thar, she blows."

Rowboats dropped into the sea. "Pull away mates," the officer shouted. The men strained against their oars.

The harpoon whizzed through the air. The whale shuddered when the steel pierced its skin. The oarsmen rowed through blood.

"No," Janie screamed. "No!"

Her own voice woke her. Her heart was thumping.

She sat up. Hugging herself, she took a deep breath, then another deeper, slower one. Hang on, hang on; it was just a dream. Her breathing evened out.

"Courtney?" Janie leaned over the edge of her bunk.

Courtney's cot was empty. Maybe she'd gone to the head.

Janie lay down again. The boat was still pitching, but the seas didn't feel as rough.

Someone came down the ladder. Janie listened to the footsteps walking past. Where was Courtney, anyway? Janie climbed out of her bunk.

In the dining room, Ralph and Steve were still asleep. Monica was gone. The door to the head had been latched open.

Outside, a bleak wet dawn crept across the sky. Water washed along the deck and sloshed back into the sea. The wind whistled around the boat.

Courtney stood at the stern. From the way her shoulders kept heaving, Janie could tell she was vomiting. It went on and on. Janie had never seen anyone as sick as that.

Courtney turned around. Limp, stringy hair stuck to her face and neck. Vomit covered her pink shirt. With both hands on the railing, she made her way along the deck.

Janie opened the door and reached out a hand. Courtney shook her head. She dropped into the first booth and crouched forward, shivering.

"I'll get a blanket," Janie said.

Courtney wiped vomit off her chin. She had tears in her eyes.

At the other end of the aisle, Vicky and Pete folded up their sleeping bags. Steve was just stirring.

"Vicky," Janie called. "Could I borrow a blanket? Courtney's sick."

Vicky and Pete came down the aisle. "Steve," Vicky said. "Go put on water for tea."

"Okay."

"Let's go," Pete said. They headed for the galley. Courtney was shivering uncontrollably now.

"We'll help you out of these clothes," Vicky said. "You shouldn't get chilled."

Quickly Janie and Vicky undressed Courtney, who was too miserable to protest. Vicky wrapped her in heavy blankets. "Janie, can you find some dry things?" She handed Janie the smelly soaked pile.

"Sure." Janie hurried below. She tossed the wet stuff on the floor and grabbed a suitcase. She didn't bother to look for stuff that matched.

By the time Janie came back, Courtney was sipping steaming hot tea. The trembling had pretty much stopped.

"Seasickness is grim," Vicky said. "The first time, I was so wiped out I wondered if throwing myself overboard wouldn't be better."

Courtney pulled the blankets around her. With her head down, she said, "I never should have come. I don't belong here."

"Oh, Courtney," Janie said, feeling awful.

"The worst is over," Vicky said. "You'll be all right now."

Other people staggered into the dining room. Ralph headed down the aisle to start breakfast.

Janie watched Steve set out cereal bowls on the galley counter. Why had he acted as if he liked her the other morning? It didn't make sense if Monica was his girlfriend. "Courtney, you want to get dressed?"

Courtney nodded, but it was a while before she stood. Janie and Vicky walked her down the aisle.

CHAPTER 11

THE dining room was crowded with whale watchers eating breakfast and talking about the storm. Janie took a roll and went out on deck.

She chewed on the plain brown bread. After a few bites, the empty unsettled feeling in her stomach eased.

Weak light filtered through the clouds. The rain had pretty much let up. The ocean lapped quietly at the hull as if there'd never been a storm, but fog had settled all around.

Sea fog was different from the kind on the lake at home. There it hovered and clung to the surface of the water. Janie closed her eyes.

Harold would be fishing on Hippo's Back by now. Fang was probably crashing around in the underbrush. The geese were lifting off in wide arching circles.

"Hi, Janie."

"Oh!" She started. "Hi, Steve."

He leaned his arms on the railing at a little distance from her and stared at the water.

She couldn't think of anything to say. Her brain felt fogged in.

"I just wanted to tell you . . . last night at supper . . ." Steve cleared his throat. "Monica always says stuff like that."

"Oh!" said Janie. It was almost as if he knew what she'd been thinking before. "When I saw you two sleeping, I figured—"

Steve blushed. Janie didn't know that could even happen to boys.

"It was a bad storm, Janie. I mopped the wheelhouse deck this morning, and there were dead fish and seaweed all over it."

"You mean waves rolled over the top deck?"

He smiled. "Must have been something to see."

"Jeez, no wonder everyone was barfing."

"Yeah, Monica was sick so many times she gave up going back to her sleeping bag. She just sat with me."

No wonder, Janie thought. "That makes sense."

Steve turned to her. "There was also a report last night that the entangled whale might be in this area."

"Really?"

"They think it's a humpback whale called Kitten's Paw. Her flukes have scars that look like cat tracks. Want to keep watch with me?"

"Okay."

The fog crept up to the bowsprit. There wasn't much to see. The *Yankee* moved steadily through gray air and gray waves.

Janie rested her elbows on the railing behind and looked starboard. Steve was standing close, like yesterday.

"Steve, where are we? I mean on a map and all."

"Directly south of Nova Scotia, between Browns Bank and Jordan Basin. We're heading toward the Maine coast."

Steve seemed like a good guy. It was probably true about Monica.

The fog swept right over the bowsprit, wrapping them in a tighter billowy mist. The only sounds came from the lapping water and the *Yankee*'s engines.

Each time the bow rose on a wave, Janie's shoulder rubbed his arm. As the boat dipped, Steve's arm pressed against hers.

"Steve, we still have one more day, right?"

"No, just till this afternoon."

"Yikes, I lost track of the days. It's going by so fast."

He slid a hand along the rail behind her. She leaned against it. His fingers settled near her waist. Those hot shivers ran all over her again.

"Janie." The heaviness of his arm felt good. He pulled her closer to him.

Steve's face was wide and full, but he had small curvy lips. His breath smelled of something minty. If she lifted her chin just a little, Janie thought, it could be like in the movies. He would kiss her.

Steve's arm jerked away. "What's that?"

"What?" She started.

A length of yellow fishnet drifted on the water. Janie heard a thrashing sound, then a whale's sigh.

"It's got to be her," he said.

"You mean right out there?"

"Yeah, I better—"

"Go!" said Janie.

Steve ran for the ladder. "Keep watching."

Janie didn't turn around even when she heard the captain and Pete step out on the wheelhouse deck. "The fog's too dense to see from here," Pete said. "I'm going below."

"Janie," the captain called. "Did you see anything, yet?"

"No—Yes! There—there she is!"

The whale lunged out of the waer. The fishnet

trailed beneath her, wrapped around both flippers. Caught in the net were beer cans and plastic detergent bottles, even two old car tires. The net vanished when she dived.

"I didn't know there'd be junk," Janie said.

"Yep," said Pete as he came to the rail. "And it's heavy to be dragging around."

A few minutes later, Steve appeared on the other side of Janie. "It'll be a while before the patrol boat gets here. I hope we can stay with her."

"What'd you mean?" said Janie. "Why wouldn't we?"

Pete looked at the fog. "Whales have a way of vanishing. Following her around could really throw us off course. The *Yankee*'s scheduled to be back in port by early afternoon. Some people have planes to catch to get back home."

"But we have to! Suppose the patrol boat can't find her out here?"

Pete nodded. "They might not."

Steve said, "My father says everyone has to vote. That's the only fair way to decide."

Janie didn't want to leave the bowsprit even though it began to rain. She pulled up the hood on her slicker and kept watching.

"I don't get it." Steve shook his head. "Don't you want to vote, Janie?"

"My vote's to stay. I'll watch out here. You guys just convince everyone else."

Pete smiled at her. "You know, Janie, in olden days, sailors got the plank for not following captain's orders."

Janie laughed. "Aye, aye, sir!"

"Ted's watching from the helm," Pete said. "Another pair of eyes won't hurt. Start yelling, Janie, if you see anything—anything at all."

"I will."

"Janie," Steve said. "I'll be watching from the wheelhouse also."

"Okay."

Janie looked at the two of them moving down the deck. "Hey—wait! Pete, tell everyone about the garbage she's dragging. Tell them how gross it is."

There was another splash. Kitten's Paw breached out of the water with the net over her back like a shawl.

"Let's go," said Pete. "We can't waste time."

Alone on the bowsprit, Janie felt a damp wind blow in her face. She shoved her hands in her pockets and leaned forward against the railing. Her feet were cold. There was nothing to see except the fog swirling above the water.

Too bad about Steve and the almost kiss, she thought. At least it wasn't like that time in second grade when she and Harold smoked cigars and then smashed their faces together to see what kissing was all about. Probably kissing didn't have to be like that. No wonder she never wanted to.

"Janie? Are you okay?"

"Hi, Mom. Sure. Did they start voting, yet?"

Mrs. Tannenbaum put her arm around Janie. "There're a few people who don't want to be late getting back."

"What are they, crazy? Who were they?"

"Just some people."

"Mom, did anyone say there might be only three hundred right whales *left*?"

"Pete did."

"How did the Kimuras vote?"

"Their whole family is for staying, but the captain said at least two-thirds have to vote yes."

"You voted for me, right?"

Janie's mother smiled. "When your name was called at least five people must have said 'yes' for you."

"Aww, right. Mom, you've got to talk to that French guy. It seemed like he cared."

"Okay, I'm going, but here're my gloves. It's freezing."

The dampness felt like a razor cutting through Janie's shoulders. She put on the gloves and counted on her fingers. Two-thirds of the vote meant twenty people. If her parents and she and Courtney and all the Kimuras voted to stay that would be eight.

"Janie?"

With an elbow on the railing Courtney guided herself up the slippery deck. In her hands were two paper cups with lids. "These are both for you. The cook said it's early, but you need something hot."

"Thanks. Any decision yet?"

"No. They're still voting."

"It's taking so long!"

Janie took one cup from Courtney and wrapped her fingers around it for warmth. "Did you vote?"

Courtney looked off at the fog. "Janie," she said sliding her nail along the lip of the other cup she was holding for Janie. "I want to go home and . . ."

Oh, no, Janie thought. "And?"

"What?" Courtney looked at her.

"You were going to say something else."

"We can't leave that whale, Janie. That'd be awful."

"Oh," Janie sighed. "Thank goodness!"

Courtney nodded.

Janie pried up the lid on her cup. "What is this?"

"I couldn't look."

"Are you feeling better?" Janie took a sip of the boiling soup. "Oh, that's good!"

"Yuk—that smell." Courtney gulped.

"I'll stand downwind of you."

"Janie, listen. There's something I have to tell you about Steve."

"Janie Tannenbaum!" The loudspeaker blared.

Janie started. "About Steve?"

The captain bellowed, "We've voted to stay with the whale."

"Yeah," Janie roared. "Hang on Kitten's Paw, we're coming. Tell me later, Courtney. Okay?"

The *Yankee*'s engines cut back. "Your attention, please." It was the captain again. "The rescue team is a mile off the port bow. If all goes well, a small inflatable boat will be approaching the whale soon."

"At last," Janie said. Her teeth were chattering. Her toes were stiff.

"Maybe we should go in," Courtney said.

"I have to see this . . . no matter what."

Whale watchers hurried out to the deck. Vicky, Pete, and Janie's mother stood along the railing.

Mrs. Tannenbaum looked at Janie. "You okay?"

"Yeah, where's Dad?"

"He's going to try to film it from the wheelhouse. The captain said he could."

Kitten's Paw splashed out of the water. The yellow

net was pressed across her mouth, over her head, and down her sides. Her flippers were pinned to her body. She vanished.

"She's panicking," Pete said. "Making it worse."

This is going to be bad, Janie thought.

"If this keeps happening to whales," Courtney said, "there won't be any left."

An ocean without whales, Janie thought. Sort of like home without cows and a lake. Home with no parents or Fang. No Harold. Not home at all.

Kitten's Paw surfaced and tried to open her mouth. The movement tightened the net that was already stretched taut over her flippers. Blood oozed out in diamond-shaped cuts and seeped into the water. The whale thrashed her flukes and dived.

If whales trembled, Janie thought, from just being touched, what could this feel like?

Courtney turned from the rail. "I don't think I can watch."

Janie glanced quickly at Courtney, then back to the water.

"Janie, the blood . . ."

"It's okay," Janie said.

Somewhere out in the fog, the whale sighed. It was a wheezy sound, more like a cough.

"What's that?" Janie said.

Vicky shook her head. "Sound's like the net's in her blowhole. She could suffocate."

"What!"

Pete banged on the railing. "Where are they? The boat should be here by now."

"There!" cried Janie.

Courtney grabbed Janie's hand. "Don't let go."

Janie pressed Courtney's small hand inside her own and kept watching.

A rubber boat with an outboard on back bounced over the water and through the mist. The man and woman in it waved their arms in the air.

The raft looked like a toy approaching the whale. Kitten's Paw slapped the water with her tail.

"Her flukes," Pete said, "could kill them."

Vicky nodded. "That's Julie and Mike out there, Pete."

"I know. I heard they were coming."

The raft moved steadily closer to the whale. Mike bent over the side. He was close enough to run a hand along the whale's head.

"Hey!" Pete shouted. "Mike got the buoys on!"

Four buoys, like orange beach balls, bobbed in the water alongside of Kitten's Paw.

"Say a prayer," Vicky said.

Janie looked at her.

110

Pete pointed.

The whale's flukes slapped the ocean. Julie and Mike fought to keep their balance as the raft rose and fell on waves the whale made. Kitten's Paw bashed the water again. The raft bounced.

"Easy, girl," said Janie. "Ea-sy."

"She's not trying to dive," Pete said. "She must be exhausted from fighting to get free."

"Is that good or bad?" Courtney asked.

"Good, if they can just get through this next part. Keep your fingers crossed."

Janie crossed as many fingers as she could. Please, please, please, she prayed.

Mike leaned out of the raft again. This time he had a clawlike hook in his hand. He tried getting hold of the net with it. The first time he missed, but the second time he got it.

Kitten's Paw leaped forward. The lightweight boat was towed along.

"She's dragging them!" Vicky shouted.

"It's okay, Vic," Pete said. "It's okay. They know what they're doing. He just has to cut very, very carefully."

Janie grimaced. "Pete! You mean he might cut her more?"

"No, but he's got to figure out where to cut the

net. If he cuts the wrong lines, she'll break away with most of it attached. She can't afford that. Not if her blowhole's covered.

Kitten's Paw swam along the surface. The raft stayed with her. As they moved, Mike kept cutting.

When he yanked up the grappling hook, a length of fish netting lifted. The whale's flippers splashed the water. Mike peeled the rest off her head.

Kitten's Paw thrashed her flukes. She dived and was gone.

"Woa!" Janie shouted. Courtney clapped, and cheers broke out all over.

"Hey, look!" Janie said. A bushy-shaped blow shot up. " 'Atta girl, Kitten's Paw!" Janie roared.

Mike and Julie waved their hands in the air. Then Julie swung the rubber boat around, and they disappeared into the fog.

The captain said, "There're hot drinks inside. We'll be heading for home, now. We're about one hundred miles off course, but we aren't too far behind schedule.

"We did it Pete," Janie said. "She's free."

"I'm concerned about that net. Some of it might still be in her blowhole. We won't know for sure that she's okay until someone sees her six months or a year from now and sends us a photograph."

"I was hoping we wouldn't have to ask her forgiveness."

"What?" said Pete. "I don't understand."

"Just an old idea about asking forgiveness from creatures you kill."

Pete shook his head. "I'm afraid we have to ask for an awful lot of forgiveness from the whales."

"I know," said Janie quietly. "That's why I was hoping Kitten's Paw would be all right."

CHAPTER 12

THE fog and clouds cleared off late in the day. Birds circled about the *Yankee*. Someone thought he spotted a great blue heron. Most of the whale watchers gathered on the deck hoping to see a few more whales before land came into view.

Janie found Courtney alone at the stern. "Hey, there! What are you doing?"

"Just fooling around." Courtney's sketch book lay open on her lap. Little boxes of pastels were on the bench beside her.

"That's neat."

Courtney's drawing caught the pale sky with its pinkish glow along the horizon. The water was more silvery than blue.

"It's so beautiful out here, Janie. The water changes so much; it's almost as if it has moods."

"You aren't still upset you came?"

"If I hadn't, I'd never have seen those whales. I just wish I hadn't been so pathetic this morning."

"What d'you mean?"

"Some great outdoor experience! I threw up in the ocean."

"Oh, come on. Nobody cares!"

"I do. I was hoping I could be braver and stronger if I did things like you."

"Me, brave?" Janie never thought of herself that way. "Courtney, you're not the only one who lost it. Steve said Monica blew her cookies. So did Ralph, and they work on board."

Courtney frowned. "Janie, listen. There's something I have to tell you."

"Okay, but you got to understand that you did do something brave. I mean, you decided to go on this trip."

"But I've been terrified."

"So! Being scared was part of the trip. You still did it."

"You think so?"

"Of course! Next time you'll be out in that little boat saving those whales single-handedly."

Courtney laughed. "No way!"

"So what was it you wanted to tell me?"

Courtney looked at her. "When I was sick this morning, Monica was out here. She and Steve are going out."

"She said that!"

Courtney nodded.

"He gave me the feeling they weren't."

"Really! What did he say?"

"That Monica always says stuff as if she's his girl-friend."

"Maybe she *was* making it up."

Janie shrugged.

"Janie, if he said something about her to you, he probably really likes you."

"Who knows! All I can tell you is this never happened with Harold."

"Janie! *Nothing's* ever happened with him."

Janie smiled. "That's not true. Once we tried kissing, but he threw up from the cigars."

"Now, Janie, that's pathetic."

"I think you're right."

All afternoon and into the early evening the *Yankee* raced south. While Courtney drew at the stern, Janie stood in the bowsprit. The ocean sparkled and shimmered with light just the way Courtney had shown it, but no whales broke the water's surface. It was hard to know what to think about Steve. Maybe all boys did stuff like that. Maybe Harold would too. Maybe, he would have a girlfriend or be married when she got back.

"Hey." Steve walked forward.

"Hi, there." Now what should she do?

"Wasn't this morning incredible?"

"Yeah."

"I watched from the wheelhouse with my father and yours."

"Oh, right. He was filming."

"Janie, I was wondering if you'd like to see the wheelhouse? It's kind of neat up there."

"Okay." He was still being really friendly.

"Usually, they don't let people up," Steve said. "It's a small area."

They climbed the ladder and crossed the upper deck. Steve unhooked the chain that separated the top deck from the wheelhouse. Janie followed him.

The view was incredible. She could see the horizon in every direction. The world looked like a very big place.

"In here, Janie." Steve opened a door.

Inside the wheelhouse, the ceiling, cabinets, and floor were made of dark shiny wood. There were dials and lights, monitors and a compass. Windows looked out on three sides.

Ted, the helmsman, stood behind a large spoked

wheel. It had the kind of handles sticking out of it that she'd seen in old sailor movies. "This is super."

"Would you like to try your hand at the wheel?" Ted asked.

"Could I?"

He nodded and stepped aside but kept one hand on the helm.

Janie rested her hands on the smooth wooden wheel. The vibrations ran up her arms and across her back.

Ted eased the wheel starboard just a little then let go. The boat shifted its course.

The *Yankee* responded like a living creature. The wheel felt alive, like a heart. "I love it. Now, I have to be a sea captain too."

"Let me take over again. We're coming up on something."

Janie let go. "Thanks." She followed Steve outside.

Below on the bow, people were pointing and shouting. "What's going on?" Steve asked his father.

The captain said, "Pete thinks they've identified one of the whales they know by name."

"Who is it?"

"Silver."

"Who's Silver?" Janie asked.

"There's this humpback," Steve said. "Years ago, half her tail was cut off by a boat's propeller but she lived."

"Jeez!"

"There she is!" Pete bellowed.

Off the port deck, a whale's tail rose out of the water. The fluke on one side was long and graceful; the other was a stump. Silver's half-tail waved. It reminded Janie of a hand with several fingers missing. The black-and-white fluke sank beneath the water.

Captain Bob said, "Silver can migrate with the other whales. She even had a calf."

"Why'd they call her Silver?"

Steve said, "After Long John Silver and his peg leg. Come on, let's go below, I'll show you photos of her."

They stood at a table in the deserted dining room. "See all these tail shots," Steve said. "Every few years someone spots her in a different location. They send us photos."

Janie pored over the different pictures. There was no mistaking Silver's distinctive tail. "It's so neat that you can keep track of her. I hope my mother got pictures of her and of Kitten's Paw."

"Would you send copies of them to me? I keep my own log of whales I've seen. I'll give you my address."

"Sure," said Janie glancing at Steve.

"Maybe we could keep in touch."

"Okay."

"Attention, everyone," the captain said. "We'll be docking in an hour."

"I can't believe it's over," Janie said. "It went so fast."

"I know." He leaned closer. "Janie, promise me, you'll write."

"I'll try," she said backing away. "I should start packing."

"Janie, wait. Here."

The porpoise tooth! She'd completely forgotten about it. "I never got it back after the talk."

"Monica found it in one of the booths."

"Maybe she should have it."

"I want you to keep it. I'll give her another one."

"Oh! Well, thanks." She hurried below.

First it was only a fuzzy tuft along the horizon. Then there were hills covered with trees. From a mile off, the town looked like a child's toy set.

"Hey," said Janie. "The drawbridge is going up for us."

"I guess I'll go get my bags," Courtney said.

"There's still time."

"I thought I'd change."

"Don't bother; you're fine."

Courtney glanced down at herself. "Yeah, maybe I won't. I like the clothes you picked out for me. I feel different in them."

With her hair pulled back and her face windburned, Courtney did seem kind of different. The fancy shirt she had on didn't go with her jeans, but so what? Why did clothing always have to match?

"Janie, I want to go thank Vicky for this morning."

"Okay. I'll see you in a little while."

Janie headed aft. She leaned against the stern railing. The vibration from the engines felt good thumping against her slightly queasy stomach. She had to be the only person in the world who got seasick after the voyage.

She took deep breaths of air and closed her eyes. The wind felt hot and dry as the boat came closer to land.

"Janie!" Steve climbed down the ladder. "I've been looking for you. Your T-shirt. We didn't have any of the blue ones left, only red." He flipped it off his shoulder and onto hers.

"Thanks," she said. "Hey, could I get an extra one?"

"Oh, for Courtney—sure." Steve leaned over and touched her cheek. "Janie . . ."

His fingers felt rough against her skin. No way, Janie thought. She stuck out her hand. "Thanks, it's been a great trip."

Steve blinked. He shook her hand. "You have to write."

"I'll try."

A few minutes later the *Yankee* docked in the harbor. A man on the pier roped the boat's lines to the cleats. The gangway was lowered.

"So long, come again," Captain Bob said as Janie and Courtney walked down.

"Thanks," Janie said. "I had a swell time."

"We did too," said Vicky. "Take good care of yourself, Courtney."

"I will."

"And Janie," Vicky said. "If I don't see your parents, tell them we all want to hear about their trip."

"Right!" said Pete. "We'll want a copy of that video of the whales courting and the entanglement."

"Okay," said Janie. "I'll tell them. Well, bye."

Janie and Courtney made their way toward the parking lot. Janie glanced back. Steve and Monica were standing at the bow, waving good-bye and laughing. They both had on blue T-shirts.

Janie shook her head. Who cared if they were or weren't girlfriend and boyfriend? It was still fun.

"Oh, Janie. Am I ever glad to be going home."

Janie spotted her parents' car across the parking lot. "I am too," she said. "Real glad."

CHAPTER 13

THE boat was rocking and pitching. Janie's stomach quivered and rolled, but something was wrong. She heard whining.

Janie opened her eyes. Two big brown eyes stared down at her. "Fang! How you doing, boy?"

The dog licked her face. She kissed him on the lips. "Did Harold take good care of you?"

Fang rolled on his back. He yipped and wiggled around.

"Is that so?" Janie scratched Fang's belly.

Last night her parents had decided to drive all the way back, even though it was late. They'd dropped Courtney off and were home by daybreak.

Janie sat up slowly. The clock said 3:00 P.M. She'd slept all day but still felt really gross.

She crawled out of bed and made her way down

the hall to the bathroom. Dropping her pajama bottoms, she sat down on the toilet. At least the toilet wasn't rocking.

She scratched her head and yawned. There were three red spots inside her pajamas.

"Oh," she said quietly. She'd gotten *it*. Those were cramps, not seasickness.

"Mom," Janie called.

"What?" her mother answered from the bedroom.

"Mom, come here."

"Janie, I can't. I'm in the middle of something."

"Mom, I need you."

Her mother was there in an instant. "Janie, what's wrong?"

"Look." Janie pointed.

"Oh, Janie! Your period."

"Yeah, how *about* that!"

Her mother's eyes filled with tears. "You're growing up."

"I thought you'd be happy."

Mrs. Tannenbaum sniffled. "I am. It's wonderful."

"So what are you crying for? Wait till Courtney hears."

Janie's mother hugged her. "I have some things in my room you can use. I'll be right back."

Janie picked up the pajama bottoms. "Mom, you want to frame these or what?"

While she waited, Janie took off her pajama top and wrapped a white towel around herself. She ran water in the tub and dumped in extra bubble bath.

In the mirror, her hair was wild and curly just the way she liked it. She held up one of the silver whale earrings Courtney had bought her in the marina gift shop. It shone against her tanned skin. Who knows? she thought, maybe sometime, just for the fun of it, she'd wear earrings.

Janie turned sideways to the mirror and peered over her shoulder. She lowered her eyelids exactly the way actresses did in the movies. "You're terrific, Janie Tannenbaum!"

After dinner Janie sat in front of her bedroom closet sorting out shoes. "Oh, man," she groaned. "I don't want to be doing this."

"Here, Fang." She flung a worn brown loafer across the room. Fang jumped off the bed and charged after it.

Janie stood and stretched. "Mom," she shouted, "I'm going over to Harold's. I haven't been able to get hold of him."

"Did you finish?" Janie's mother called from her room.

Janie looked around at the piles of school clothing on her bed and the stacks of old toys on the floor. "Ahh, not quite."

"Janie," Mrs. Tannenbaum said coming down the hall, "you promised you'd help once we got back from vacation."

"I will. I just want to thank Harold for taking care of Fang."

"Don't be long. We have tons of work to do."

"Okay. Come on, Fang."

Janie headed out the back door. The world was still rolling and pitching a bit. Her father had said that happened after being on the ocean for almost a week. He'd blushed when she dropped the news that it *wasn't seasickness.*

Fang ran ahead of her across the lawn. Red and orange tinged the trees. The air smelled of damp soil and ripe blackberries.

Down by the lake a flock of geese squawked. Geese had a way of knowing when to head south, just like whales.

No one answered the Wazby's front door even after she rang the bell seven times. She threw pinecones at Harold's window. "Rats." Where was he?

As she turned to leave, reedy music floated through the twilight coming from Hippo's Back. It had to be him.

Cutting between the pine trees, Janie saw Harold on the tip of the rock. She stood still.

His flute music went with sunset. It was quiet and almost sad. The last of the light sank behind the trees. In the marsh, where the mud was thick and oozy, the old bullfrog croaked out his love song.

Harold lowered his flute. He rubbed his lips.

"Hi," she said slipping in beside him. "Thanks for taking care of Fang. He told me he had a real good time at your house."

"Sure thing."

Harold stood. "Listen, I have to go." He started toward the woods.

"Harold?" Janie followed him.

He didn't look at her. Instead, he fiddled with the flute's mouthpiece.

"Why didn't you come over? I asked your sister to tell you we were home."

"I knew. I dropped off Fang early this morning."

"Are you angry or something?"

Harold looked off at the water.

Okay, I give up, Janie thought. She turned to leave. "Fang!"

"You didn't even say good-bye, Janie."

"What?"

"When you went on vacation, you just left."

"It was the middle of the night. I opened your back door and let Fang in."

"Yeah, well. I didn't like it."

Harold had never talked like that before. She didn't know what to say.

"And now you're leaving again?"

"In a week."

"For a whole year."

"Yeah, but aren't we going to write?"

"You never did when you went into the hospital, Janie."

"Jeez, I was ten years old!"

Harold shrugged.

"Aren't you going to come to the dances at Courtney's school?"

"You want me to?"

"Of course. And can't I come visit you and milk the cows?"

"If you want."

"What'd you think?"

"I don't know."

"Oh, come on." Janie laughed. "Here. This is for you."

Harold held up the red T-shirt. There was just enough light to see the two whales. "Hey," he said. "Neat."

"Yeah, I have one too."

"Right whales?"

"You know that?"

"I'm the one who told you about whales in second grade."

"Oh, I forgot that." She tossed him a small white bag. "This too."

He opened it. *"Moby Dick."*

"To read to the cows when I visit."

He gave her a funny little smile.

"I found it in the gift shop before we started home. I wanted to bring you something from our trip."

"But why? It's your birthday soon, not mine."

"Just like that. I don't know."

"Fang missed you. He whined a lot and didn't eat much while you were gone."

"Yeah, I missed him. You too."

"So, did you see any whales or what?"

"Yeah! Right whales, sperm whales, dolphins, humpbacks, finbacks—you name it."

"No kidding."

"Really. You stand there on the bowsprit. It's kind of like this." She outlined the shape of Hippo's Back with her finger. "Whales and sharks come right up."

"Jeez, sharks too!"

"Yeah, thirty feet long and whales the size of a school bus. Harold, you should see them jumping. Some even have names."

"Janie! I have to go up to my house for a second. Wait here, okay?"

"Want me to come with you?"

"No, I'll be right back."

Janie stood on the tip of Hippo's Back. The bowsprit and Steve had been fun and all. Probably she'd go on other whale watches, but she needed to milk a whole bunch of cows first.

The sky had turned dark. A new moon was rising. The sticky air had gone chilly.

Fang broke through the underbrush. Harold was right behind him. "Here, I got this for your birthday, but I want to give it to you now."

Janie sat down. Fang stretched out next to her. "What is it?" She opened the folder.

"I sent your name in to this place. You get to adopt a whale. They'll send you pictures and news about sightings for the one you pick."

"Oh, Harold."

There were pictures of whales with all kinds of names like Cloud and Flag and Buckshot and Spoon. There was even a picture of Kitten's Paw with the cat tracks across her tail. Silver, the whale with the severed fluke, wasn't there, but her calf, named Coral, was shown.

Tears welled up in Janie's eyes. A lump caught in her throat. She leaned her head against Harold's shoulder so he couldn't see.

"Hey," he said. "You okay?"

"Yeah."

"You seem different."

"Nope, I'm just me." Janie wiped her nose on her sleeve.

A breeze rustled in the trees and made ripples on the lake. She shivered.

Harold said, "You want my sweater?"

"Nah."

Harold took off his sweater anyway. He put it over her shoulders.

"Thanks." She snuggled into the bulky warmth of it. She liked the way it smelled of him.

Harold slipped his arm around her.

"Harold!" Janie pulled back. "You know what I want to do before I leave?"

"What's that?"

"Let's try *Moby Dick* on the cows." She felt his arm pulling her closer. "I want to see if—"

Harold mumbled something.

"What did you say?"

"I said," said Harold, "shut up, Janie Tannenbaum."

Her laughter danced out across the water. An owl hooted back from the darkness.

Harold tilted his head toward hers. This time Janie was ready for the feel of his warm soft lips when she lifted her face. A shooting star raced across the sky just before she closed her eyes, but after that, she barely heard the bluegills jumping or the bullfrogs serenading, it was so much fun kissing Harold.

AFTERWORD

THIS book was written in memory of Silver, the amazing humpback that dazzled whale watchers and researchers for more than a decade. She was first seen in Cape Cod waters in 1978. After that, she gave birth to five calves. Beltane, her 1980 calf, had a calf in 1985, making Silver a grandmother.

In the spring of 1991, Silver was found dead, entangled in a gill net off Long Island, New York. Her life tells the story of generations of humpback whales.

Losing an old friend is always sad. I hope that Silver's offspring may someday have the freedom to wander throughout the oceans of the world unharmed and protected as international citizens. There is always hope for wishes to come true.

Natalie F. R. Ward
Humpback Whale Researcher